Those Old Women:
Tell their stories

To Alice
God's Woman
may you succeed
in your ministry as
Pastoring God's
people

Sheila
Robinson
10/4/2018

1

Those Old Women: Tell their stories

ISBN-13:978-1534672437
ISBN-10:1534672435

CONTENTS

Scriptural References

Introduction

My visits to countries outside of the United States have been enriching beyond measure and responsible to some degree for the expansion of my understanding of how other people in various parts of the world live and experience life. But still, I am by no means an expert on the ways of life, culture, and mores of the indigenous people I met during my visits to their countries. I can only draw a very minimal conclusion of how and why they live as they do. These conclusions are based very loosely on structured and primarily prearranged periods of interaction and visitation between them and me. And by the very same token, non-residents of the US who visit for selected periods of time cannot declare themselves experts on the cultures, practices and dialects of the people and citizenry of the United States. A traveler to America for example who visits the wealthy and opulent areas of Hollywood cannot conclude that the entire American population lives that same lavish and sumptuous lifestyle.

It is for these reasons and more that readers and serious scholars of the Scriptures should exercise caution when claiming to be experts concerning the lives of the women of Biblical antiquity. We have come to know them only vicariously through the expressions of mostly male writers who did not live the same experiences of the women about whom they wrote. Hence, we know the women of Biblical literature on a very superficial level. We learned of their plights via the scripting of someone(s) other than themselves, writings of others who claimed to have sufficient enough knowledge about them to write their stories. The storylines were most likely documented without benefit of personal narratives from the women who lived them. This novel takes a look into the lives and experiences of a few women in the Scriptural text with whom we have some degree of familiarity, and explores the probability of what these women might say if given the opportunity to speak for themselves.

With that in mind, this book is dedicated to women everywhere through all time. To the women in the inner cities, women in the glamorous fast-paced cities, women in the forgotten cities and the lost ones, the unknown cities, the wealthy cities, the suburbs, the fashion capitols, the outbacks, the small towns, the ghettos, the urban communities, the jungles, the rain forests, the deserts, and the mountains; to women wherever they happen to be, this book is dedicated to you.

To the women who have been hopeful, helpful, worn, abused, tortured, enslaved, loved, respected, disrespected, destroyed, dejected, reviled, revered, worshipped, and ignored; to the ones who are or have been fearful, tearful, dreadful and hateful, to those who are vengeful, careful, pitiful, mindful, willful, tasteful, prayerful, powerful and beautiful, this book was written with you in mind and is dedicated to your tenacity and your resolve.

This dedication carries with it a salute to the strength of every woman who has had to endure more than she should. It honors the women who have had to carry more than their share; it speaks to their legacy and their fortitude, it cherishes their victories and their failures. This book is dedicated to the memory of every woman through-out all time.

Chapter 1
They Came to Tell Me

Jennifer sat with her publisher in the office of a major publishing company which had expressed a strong interest in her story. The publishing company, New World Writers Publishing, (NWWP) felt Jennifer's narrative was a provocative fictional mystery with mass appeal across ethnic and cultural boundaries and wanted to conduct one more final read before going to print. Jennifer's head was whirling with myriad emotions from hopefulness to anxiety, mixed with amazement that she was finally here in the office of the publisher about to relinquish what she considered her personal and private treasured gem but which she was compelled to share.

Because her story centered on the lives of women, specifically those of Scripture, Jennifer felt particularly cautious about exposing her manuscript. Having been raised in a very rigid and inflexible Pentecostal church, Jennifer remembered all too well the stings and biases of gender discrimination. She bore the emotional scars of that powerful indoctrination. Though secretly not accepting the dogma of female inferiority nor the teaching that such gender lowliness had been ordained of God from the beginning of time, she nonetheless had found no one within her religious community to talk to about her thoughts. Her internal struggle had remained her own personal and private conflict. And while every sermon and every story she had heard concerning women of the Scriptures had been presented through the lens of masculine interpretation, still Jennifer often wondered how the accounts might have unfolded had the women themselves been given an opportunity to tell their own stories. Well finally, the details of that speculation were now contained in the flash-drive she clutched in her nervous and moist hand. It was a written documentation of her face-to-face encounter with the women of the far and distant past who had shared with her their painful personal experiences as they had lived through them. But it was the distorted manner by which these stories had been told, retold, and accepted as Scriptural truths read by millions throughout time, that most disturbed these women.

Slowly and with trepidation Jennifer released her grip on the flash-drive and handed it over to the publisher who was prepared to make the final read. Placing the flash-drive into the computer, the publisher opened the document and began to read Jennifer's chronicle. It began...

I am forever changed since that night. I will never forget them, I can't. This unique group of women who dropped in on me unexpectedly one night, without prior notice or invitation, captured my attention, changed my thinking, and influenced me for always. It all happened just recently. The day itself had been fairly typical, rather uneventful, not bearing the slightest hint of what was to come later that night.

After completing my nightly reading and turning off my bedside lamp, I settled into bed, sank contentedly onto my new mattress, and snuggled beneath the warmth of my down comforter. I took in a deep breath and let out a long relaxing sigh as my eyes roamed my room and soaked in the soft, blue-white light of the full moon which had invaded the darkness of the night and now bathed my room in its peaceful glow. I felt myself floating in that semi-awake state just before entering the world of sleep, when suddenly I heard a voice, no...voices, many soft, gentle whispering voices floating through my room. Realizing I was still awake, I sat straight up in my bed to see who had come into my room, into my house. And interestingly enough, I was completely unafraid at the knowledge of strangers in my house and further, I was prepared to confront them. Who were they, how had they gotten in, and why were they whispering?

"Is she awake?"

"Yes, I think so."

"She looks asleep."

"But she is not."

"Are you sure?"

"Yes, look, her eyes are open."

"Maybe we should not have come."

"Of course we should."

"We have to tell her."

"Do you think she will listen to us?"

"Yes, of course."

"How can you be so sure?"

"Oh, she will."   "I think she hears us."

"Look, I think she sees us."

"She doesn't seem the least bit frightened."

"That is good."

"She is a brave soul."

Simultaneously they were all whispering in unison back and forth to each other, yet I distinctly heard and understood their separate expressions as if they were each speaking individually and one at a time. Poised at the foot of my bed, they stood together, gathered like a choir prepared to sing. With kind, peaceful smiles on their faces, they greeted me in harmony, "Good evening my dear." Still uncertain of what was going on, I thought I should ask them who they were and what they were doing in my house. But I didn't. Instead, I heard myself answer, "Hello."

This time as they began to speak, they did so one at a time, and in un-whispered tones. They said they had traveled a long, long journey, from a distance so great it could not be determined by linear measurements, but rather by degrees of time. They had come from as far back as the Garden of Eden, up through the earthly time of Jesus the Christ and finally all the way into my present. They said God had granted them permission to travel through time and conditions in order to spend an evening with me and talk to me about life, and in particular their own individual, personal lives.

Each one of them had experienced quite a unique life and felt that it was time for their truths to be heard. Clearly, their stories had been documented in Scripture, and re-told, even preached many times over during the fleeting centuries. But the writers of Scripture had not consulted them for accuracy, so it was now time for them to tell their own accounts of what had occurred many millennia ago. It was time for them to tell the meaningful ways their personal experiences had impacted them. They each seated themselves, some on my bed, some on the floor others on my chaise. I didn't know any of their names, but one by one, these distinguished women-of-biblical-antiquity, thousands of years old, introduced themselves as they began their stories. The first one began to speak.

Chapter 2
The First One

When the first woman opened her mouth to speak, she began by going back to the very beginning of time as humanity understands time. She said that, far, far, very far back in time when nothing existed outside of the mind of God, He, in His all-knowingness decided to transfer out from His own imaginative thought, some of His creative ideas into a more tangible existence. He wanted something touchable, visible and substantive. So, He expressed His will through the creation of an assemblage of spheres and matter, of space and atmosphere, of formations, reactions, gases and lights. Unique in their configuration, these entities were diverse in their essence and were comprised of various consistencies, colors, sizes, temperatures and weights having become viable substances whirling, spinning and rotating in unique patterns of movement. Visually amazing, breathtaking and beautiful, these spheres and formations danced and hung on nothingness according to the masterful, creative expression of God. And when humankind first began to look to the sky and all that the sky revealed, sheer amazement was the understandable result of what they encountered. And in an effort to keep in touch with and document their discoveries, these human explorers gave names to their discoveries. The galaxy, the universe, stars, and planets are some of the names they ascribed to God's magnificent handiwork. "But forgive me, I'm getting ahead of myself," the first speaker said. Apologizing, she confessed that she always gets very excited when speaking about the wondrous works of her God. So she continued her narrative returning back to the subject of God's creation process.

God's further, more interactive handiwork was made visible when He took a minuscule portion of His own likeness and image, combined it with a collection of meticulously arranged sub-microscopic particles which He called atoms and blended them to formulate a self-propagating, self-determining human construct to whom He gave the name Adam. Adam, comprised of millions of atoms, was a human who had been formed from the rich red, dark-brown soil of this beautiful sphere we call Earth. Into Adam, God placed boundless intellect and countless emotions. And for Adam's perpetuation and survival God provided every possible necessity for self-sufficiency, comfort, prosperity, increase and expansion to occupy the Earth sphere which had been designed specifically for human habitation. Bringing completion to His creative design God breathed His own powerful breath-of-life into Adam so that the journey of human existence as a living soul would begin with Adam. And finally so that Adam's reality could be thorough and balanced, God created me. He gave me a uniqueness that made Adam and I completely and structurally compatible and suited for each other as complementary counterparts one to the other. My name is Eve, my wonderful husband gave me my name.

On the day of my awakening I opened my eyes for the first time to behold a sight which I never have forgotten, a sight that completely filled my vision. There in front of me were the two loveliest, deep-brown, round objects speaking silently to me with a gentle tenor of wonder, affection and expectation. They embraced me and pulled me right into their space. I was transfixed, wondering what these beautiful things could be, so perfectly round, so tender and inviting. I felt myself being drawn into the excitement of their existence as waves of warmth filled me. Then surges of unexplainable feelings began to arise from deep within my being, fluttering ever so gently throughout myself, upward, downward, in circles and in every direction inside me. I seemed to be soaring and spinning, yet motionless at the same time; and all the while my gaze remained locked onto those two beautiful round objects in my sight which seemed to express an exactness of what I was feeling. We existed like that as one entity for quite some time, feeling and experiencing the same things at the same time.

Then I heard the voice of my Creator, my Perfect and Wonderful God as He softly nudged me out of my hypnotic euphoria. I knew immediately who He was, because I had previously already existed in His mind. He gently lifted me from where I lay on the ground into a sitting position and introduced me, "*Behold your husband and mate, Adam.*" As I sat there on the ground, I turned to meet Adam and saw again what I had seen when I first opened my eyes, those two beautiful round pools of glistening brown shimmer, surrounded by yet another perfectly round encircling soft-white outer shell. They were my husband's eyes, my husband Adam's captivating, big brown eyes. I would have been content to stare into the depth of his eyes for all eternity had I not caught a glimpse of the rest of him. I felt suddenly light-headed and faint, as he was too wonderful to look at. Every part of his being was supple yet rugged and beautiful. His color was identical to that of the ground upon which we sat, richly dark, and deeply reddish-brown. The hue of his being with glistening highlights and flecks of radiance dancing all over him was soothing to my eyes. I reached out to touch this magnificent husband of mine and lightly shuddered when I felt the strength of his splendid form beneath my fingertips. I searched for the voice of God to ask Him what was happening, and what was to come next with this exquisite husband He had just given me. But before I could speak my question to God, I heard Adam's voice. His voice was as hypnotic as his eyes as he spoke to me with a gentle entreating tone which urged me to follow to whatever places he would bid me come. I had no idea where I would go with Adam I just knew that I would go. He told me he was a man and that the moment he awoke and saw me he knew I was his wo-man whom God had promised. He said God had spoken to him about being alone and assured him it would not be a good thing because his aloneness would soon erode into loneliness. So God instructed Adam to go to sleep assuring him that when he awoke he would find his companion beside him. Adam said the moment he awoke he leaned over to gaze upon me and instantly became mesmerized by my eyes. He said he could see all the beauty and loveliness of my being through the intensity and depth of my eyes, and that he felt a longing to submerge himself into my presence and become one with me. He too would have been content to glare forever into my eyes had not the kind voice of our God offered us our official introduction of who we were individually and who we were in relationship to each other. God told us that to solidify the bond between us He had used one of Adams ribs as the formative core of my design, and built my flesh around it. Adam and I were both warmed and comforted by the knowledge that I possessed one of his ribs. It was for that reason Adam told me I was flesh of his flesh and bone of his bone.

Adam and I loved each other profoundly and often spent long hours exploring the wonders and fascination of ourselves as we touched each other countless times in a day. I was eager to recapture the light-headedness I felt on the day I looked at his whole being and touched him for the first time. I enjoyed experiencing that ever so slight shudder each time I stroked him. I loved touching Adam not only with my fingers and hands but with my lips as well. His lips were full, soft and sweet as I pressed against them with my own. I was delirious with touching Adam with my lips whether on his lips or wherever else on his person I fancied doing so. However, I very quickly discovered that at certain times, the warm softness of his usually downward facing appendage, transformed itself into a rigid firmness that slowly and deliberately rose upward into an upright position like a strong, rigid tower standing erect and alone as if in search for and in anticipation of something yet to come. We engaged one another during those times in exciting embraces as Adam submerged his firm tower into me, and I willingly and enthusiastically welcomed his submersion. We moved and swayed in rhythmic motions as all our senses joined in together and became concentrated on that wonderful and magnificent event of the moment.

At this point in Eve's narration Jennifer wondered if she was hearing and understanding Eve correctly. Was Eve describing her lovemaking with Adam? Interestingly enough Jennifer had never before given much thought to lovemaking between Adam and Eve even though the Scriptures are clear in saying that Adam knew his wife Eve. But hearing Eve's description of her first lovemaking experience with Adam brought a whole new and refreshing perspective to the subject of lovemaking. It sounded so perfectly pure and so very right. Sensing Jennifer's thoughts, Eve responded. Yes Jennifer, it was so perfectly pure and so very right; but since that time and for countless millennia all the way into your 21st century, humanity has made coming together for the expression of love quite profane, distorted, common, and sometimes degrading. It has become not at all like the beautiful experience our God intended it to be.

Eve then went on with her delightful unfolding of the life and events of the First Family in the Garden of Eden, the beautiful Garden of God. During the other waking hours of our days she said, we spent our time leisurely exploring the magnificence and color of the lush habitat that was our home. Green was the predominate color, I had the distinct feeling green was our God's favorite color. Almost everything was green intricately enhanced by the numerous variances in shades and hues from deep blue green to lighter yellow green to bright startling green and every tint in between. And other colors abounded. Bright, deep, tinted, swirled, spotted, speckled, striped and blended colors surrounded us everywhere like a blanket of splendor inviting us to touch, smell, taste, and visually enjoy them simply because they were there. The sky was bright and blue and expansive like an opening to another place. The sun was warm and nourishing. The ground beneath us was soft yet firm and presented us each morning with delicate misty dew which was soon dissipated by the early morning sun. The soft breezes danced gently around us daily and spoke tenderly to us in whispered tones. The rivers and streams invited us to join them as we splashed in joyful merriment, or floated in tranquil silence. Animals of every kind often accompanied us on our walks. The birds flitted along above us introducing us to their newest melodies of worship to our God. We ate delicious berries and fruits, drank the juices of their substance and quenched our taste for cool refreshing water from the brooks along the ways. The dark and majestic night skies revealed a numberless array of twinkling, bright objects which seemed suspended on nothingness. Adam and I usually fell asleep trying to count them. The night skies were also accompanied by a huge yellow-white sphere which changed its shape, its brightness and its placement in the sky almost nightly. Eden was the name of our estate and we loved it, after-all, it was the Garden of God.

One morning as we gathered our first meal of the day, a long, cylindrical animal approached me with a suggestion that I try something new and tasty from a different tree. He disputed what God had told Adam about the outcome of eating from this particular tree. He said we would not die as God said we would. The animal seemed friendly like all the other animals and he seemed knowledgeable about what he was telling me, implying that he had a close working relationship with our God. I was convinced by the sincerity of his conversation and the subtly of his approach, thus I concluded he was being truthful. In retrospect, I should have been alerted when his account of eating from that tree was in direct opposition to what our God had said. But alas, I succumbed to his charm and tasted the fruit. I shared it with Adam and he ate also. No sooner had we eaten, Adam and I immediately felt and sensed something we had never felt before. Those feelings were foreign to us; they were unfamiliar feelings of discomfort and shame. For the first time ever we hung our heads, we looked away from each other and had a strange sense that we were unclothed and needed to be covered. We quickly gathered some of the large leaves from one of the fig trees and entwined them together to make panels to hide parts of ourselves that we suddenly felt should not be exposed.

Our usual evening talk with the voice of God was just moments away and for the first time we dreaded it. That special time of sweet communion had always been the highlight of our day but now we were feeling something entirely new. We were afraid. As we heard God's voice walking toward us, our fear mounted causing us to run and hide in a nearby thicket among a cluster of trees. God's voice which had always been comforting and inviting now sounded forceful and scolding as He called out inquiring of Adam's whereabouts, *"Adam, where you?"* Adam and I were shaking so much we thought the rustling of our fig leaves against the thicket might reveal our hiding place. But rustling leaves notwithstanding, there is no hiding place from God. We should have remembered that, but we were afraid and fear brings about very strange behavior. Adam responded to God's inquiry with, "When I heard your voice coming to us, I saw that I was naked and I was afraid, so I hid myself from you." Although Adam spoke it, I too felt it, we were both afraid. It was the only explanation we could offer, we were afraid and we realized we were naked thus we hid. The word naked was a strange and unknown word that we had never used before. But now it seemed appropriate. God was upset with us firing questions at us like, how did we know we were naked, and did we eat from the forbidden tree. Our heads were spinning and Adam quickly explained that he ate because I gave it to him. God then looked to me and I responded that I ate on the suggestion of the serpent. Our explanations did not appease God and He proceeded to mete out punishments beginning with the serpent. God took away the serpents legs so that the only manner by which he could move about was flat on his belly with his face in the dust of the ground. God told him he was the most cursed of all animals and there would be a distinct hatred from that day forward between serpents and women. And it was at the exact moment our God uttered that castigation that I instantly felt the most bitter loathing and abhorrence for the serpent. He became immediately detestable and disgusting in my sight as I watched him slither away without his legs.

Then God turned to me and pronounced the consequence of my action. He said that bringing forth children into our world would be accompanied by much pain. In addition, God said my attraction for Adam would now intensify to the extent of becoming an almost insatiable desire for him. And finally that Adam and I would no longer reside together as two equals of differing and complimentary genders, but that Adam would wield a ruling dominion over me; God told me, *"He shall rule over you!"* Then God's final disciplinary move was toward Adam. God said the ground which had up to this point been soft and yielding in its firmness would now become antagonistic to us and begrudging in its giving of herbs and all other plant life. In so doing, sundry plants would now bring forth prickly thorns to pierce and hurt us thereby making our harvesting burdensome. Other inedible more resilient vegetation designed specifically to choke out the life of the edible foliage would grow stronger, hardier, and side by side with our productive crops. And finally, God told Adam, *"Because of your decision to ignore my command that you were not to eat any of the fruit from the tree of knowledge of good and evil, you will surely die, just as I said you would. And when you do, you will become dust again, just as you were before I first formed you from it. From dust you were formed, and to dust you shall return again. That is what the future holds for you."* But the worst of all was God's decision to forcefully eject Adam and me from our beautiful Eden, our luxuriant, blossoming, lush garden of God that we knew as Eden. Eden had been our home; it was all that we had ever known.

But then, there we were, on the outside of our beautiful Eden looking onto the fierce and unyielding countenance of the giant Cherubim guarding the east boundary of Eden. In his hand he held a huge flaming sword which turned in all directions and gave out the most intense heat forcing Adam and I to move quickly and far away from him; otherwise we would have been destroyed completely by the flames of his sword. Saddened and downcast, Adam and I understood immediately that we would never again walk along the sloping banks of our tranquil rivers in Eden, or enjoy the tasty fruit from our bountiful trees, or eat anymore of the full and plump variety of berries that grew everywhere our eyes could see. Not knowing what to do or where to go, we just sat down on a soft patch of green moss because we desperately wanted to remain as close as possible to our lovely first home; yet we knew we needed to be quite far enough away from that deadly Cherubim and his blazing sword. He seemed only too eager to strike us with it. We sat and stared at each other, then all around at our strange and unfamiliar surroundings. As we sat and stared, I noticed something on Adams face that I had not ever seen before. Small pools of water had filled his eyes and were spilling out onto his face in a linear cord running down the entire length of his stunning face and meeting under his chin. As I continued to look at him, my own vision became blurred and I felt something warm and wet making its way down the front of my face. I reached out and took Adams face in my hands and began to kiss the linear cords on his face while at the same time he cupped my face in his hands and began kissing the warm spots on my face. We sat there kissing each other's face in our attempt to understand what was happening to us with this warm water flowing from our eyes. Many years later, I learned that these pools and cords of water were known as tears. They would come into existence whenever pain, sadness, sorrow or sometimes joy were present. So, here we were, sitting and wondering. After a while from sheer emotional exhaustion, we lay down, covered ourselves with the animal skins God made for us, and fell asleep in this strange new place away from the only home we had ever known; Eden, the beautiful and tranquil Garden of our God.

When we awoke the following morning after a night that seemed very long indeed, much longer than any of our previous nights, Adam and I somehow felt very disconnected. We looked at each other as though we were seeing each other for the first time, but without the same titillation, excitement and wonder we felt when we looked upon each other for the real first time back in Eden where our God first formed us. We experienced yet again, a new feeling; there was a tension and friction in the atmosphere and an uneasiness with each other that remained with us all our living days on Earth. We had endured so much the previous day that it seemed our lives were beginning anew

27

all over again. And as we took in the sights around us in our new home, we realized that despite it being a beautiful garden, it was still not our Eden. We filled our days doing the similar things we did in Eden, but the breezes were not as soft and soothing, the waters were not as tranquil, the sun was not as bright, and the ground was not as soft nor as warm. When in Eden we never needed to look before stepping because everywhere we stepped was plush and comfortable. But now we had to be mindful of where we placed our feet when we walked because the ground was prickly and uncomfortable with vegetation that sometimes pierced our feet; and there were sharp rocks and slippery stones which often caused us to lose our footing. And our food became much more difficult to harvest.

Adam and I continued to enjoy touching and exploring each other's bodies as we had done before but now there was a slight nervousness about our coming together. It was still quite pleasurable, but there was definitely more tension than had previously been. After a while I began to feel uncomfortable at the slightest turn. My insides would often feel unsettled during the early mornings, and the middle of my body seemed to be getting fuller around as the days passed. Then one day I felt a slight flutter inside me and I didn't know what to think because it too was a new experience, and since so many new things had been happening after leaving Eden I reasoned this flutter was just another new experience. Later that same day, I felt a few more flutters and I became aware that this fluttering inside me was indeed in need of an explanation. So, I sought our God to inquire of Him about what was going on inside me. God told me He was giving me a child, a male child, the same type of human as my husband Adam, but much smaller. So I decided to give the name Cain to my man-child, because I had gotten him from the Lord. But I needed more details from our God about what He meant when He said He was giving me a child. He explained, and I was so comforted after my conversation with Him. He was so very gentle in His tone and explanation of what was going on inside of me. He said that I would be the mother of all human beings of this earth, and that I was the first woman on this earth to bring forth a child from within herself. Our God further explained that when He formed me He had purposely created a particular place within me that would be the source of fertile ground needed for a child to grow from a seed into a fully completed human person, yet much smaller than Adam and I; and without many of the abilities that Adam and I possessed. God said Adam and I would be required to take care of the small human to protect it and help it grow until it grew to become the same in size that Adam and I were. I was amazed by this information and inquired of our God as to where the seed came from and how it made its way into me. Was it a seed from a fruit or vegetation that I had eaten; and had I swallowed it along with the fruit and vegetation that I had eaten? Our God told me that was not the case, He said that seeds from fruit and vegetation can only re-produce and grow new fruit or vegetation of its own kind. He said when He created the earth and all that is in it, He determined that all of the earth's plant and animal life would contain seeds within themselves which are identical to themselves, so that each of those living things could bring forth more of themselves. And so it was that Adam and I also had many, many seeds within us so we could bring forth more humans like ourselves and continue to do so numerous times during our lives. What I could not understand at first was that in order for Adam and me to bring forth another human like us, we needed a seed from Adam and a seed from me to join together with each other, transform itself from two seeds into one seed, and be planted in my fertile place to grow. But I needed more of God's explanations, because I didn't know how our two separate seeds from our separate bodies could come together and end up planted in my fertile place. If our seeds were inside of us, how then were we to get the seeds to come from one of us and go to the other? God explained further. He reminded me that when Adam and I came together to touch and kiss and place his tower in me, his seed would leave his body through the canal within his tower, find one of my seeds and enter it just as Adam had entered me. Then the two seeds which had joined together to become one would make its way to my fertile place and plant itself there to grow. God told me that a planting had already happened and the seed had grown to the point of moving about in my fertile place and that was the fluttering I was feeling. God further said that I would continue to get much fuller in my middle and the fluttering would become much stronger until the new human was mature enough to leave me and come to live with us outside of my body. My final question to God about this matter was how the new human would get out to come live with us. God answered that my fertile place would gently push him out through the same passage by which Adam had entered me with his tower.

So there I was, about to bring forth another person into the world, someone with whom Adam and I could share this earth and begin the process of multiplying and replenishing the earth as dictated by our God. Shortly after my talk with God, Cain was born and for the very first time ever, I experienced a physical hurt that I had not ever felt before. In the long and travailing moments that accompanied the birth of Cain, I was forced to recall what God had spoken to me in Eden after our encounter with the serpent, when God looked straight into my eyes and said, "*I will greatly increase your pangs in childbearing; in pain you shall bring forth children.*" It was indeed an almost unbearable pain, but it seemed to very quickly disappear when I looked upon the

30

soft, small face of my man-child for the first time. And when I touched him, kissed him, cradled him and pressed him close to me, I felt yet again, a brand new feeling; one of an overwhelming and deep love and concern for this little creature who was not like anything I had ever seen before. He was my first-born, and he was everything good and warm.

It was so delightful to watch him grow bigger and taller and to have talks with him as the three of us learned to understand each other and respond back to one another in words which finally made some sense. Soon I noticed I was getting full around the middle again, so I reasoned another seed had been planted and was in the process of growing inside me just as Cain had grown. In the fullness of time our second, another man-child was brought into our world, and I named him Abel.

There came a time however when I was greatly distressed. It was after my first-born Cain killed his brother Abel in a murderous rage over a discrepancy concerning their offerings to God. In God's observation of the offerings presented to Him by Cain and his brother Abel, God expressed displeasure about Cain's offerings while on the other hand voiced pleasure and acceptance of Abel's offerings. Cain became enraged at this and in a fit of anger took his brother Abel's life after luring him out into a field. I don't think I ever completely recovered from the torment of my first-born having taken the life of his younger brother. But life on this earth continued and I did have another son whom I named Seth, as well as many more children. Yet, despite other children, I would never forget my second-born son Abel.

Adam and I lived long, full, prosperous lives and witnessed the birth of many children born to our children and to their children and to theirs. And so, long after Adam and I had died and returned to the same dust from which our God made us, as I roamed one day in the realm-of-the-dead moving about with no particular purpose or destination, I heard His voice again. My excitement at hearing Him after so long was too intense for me to describe now in words, but I immediately knew His voice. There was no question that it was Jesus. I knew Him, I remembered Him, I had been with Him in eternity when I existed only in the mind of God before God re-shaped me into a tangible being. Jesus had been there too, always there existing as One with God, as God. But now He was visiting me again in the realm-of-the-dead. I felt again the peace and love I first felt in Eden. Jesus told me He forgave me of my transgression of disobedience against our God. He assured me that although God had punished Adam and me for our actions, God had never stopped loving us. That it was His deeply abiding love for us which caused Him to provide for us so that we could survive and progress in the world outside of Eden. Then, Jesus told me He had just relinquished His life on a cross as an act of redemption for all of humanity. He said further that His mission now was a three-day visitation to the realm-of-the-dead to release from captivity the countless numbers of people who had died before His sacrificial act of redemption by way of His crucifixion on the cross. His presence here now was to allow everyone to retroactively benefit from His completed act of salvation. While I was happy for all those who would benefit from His 3-day visit, my only desire was to remain with Him forever and go with Him to wherever he was going. He told me that was not possible right then but assured me He would return again at a later time and would take me at that time back to eternity with Him to be once again with our God. So…I wait. He said he would return and I know He will keep His word.

Chapter 3
The Day of the Fire

Fire was everywhere, on the ground, in the air, and in the sky. Everything was on fire and burning with a ferocious intensity. The sky, just an hour ago, had been as cloudless and clear as crystal and as blue as the most tranquil ocean. But now, that same sky had become a teaming row of mountainous billowy dark gray clouds, mixed with volcanic like masses of fiery red and orange eruptions. White-hot coals and unusually large cinders were flying in every direction and exploding into numerous bursts of crimson flames. The eerie sound of cracking wood and burning trees was deafening. The threatening sounds of collapsing rocks, and crumbling bricks was unceasing. Water, from wells, streams and rivers having been heated beyond boiling was scalding everything in its path and hissing onto everything it touched before drying up into whimpering, diminishing, puffs of steam.

Two, very prosperous and thriving cities, Sodom and Gomorrah were being deliberately and methodically destroyed. Once teaming with activity, commerce and life, these cities were being reduced to a mere memory; absolutely nothing would be left of what once existed as the prosperous cities of Sodom and Gomorrah. The caved-in, sunken ground would bear no conceivable resemblance that trees once grew there, that buildings once stood there, nor that people at one time lived, worked and walked there. The ground would be forever in mourning and would never recover. It would be several months before even the wind would dare whisper itself across the remains of these cities.

In the process of this massive, unbelievably destructive outburst, about ¾ of a mile outside the borders of the cities, the mournful, lamenting thoughts of a woman all alone could be heard. I was that woman, and this is how my experience unfolded.

I felt such an indescribable pain…oh God…the pain…the pain…it was unbearable. My legs were so heavy, they felt like they were fastened to a mountain of bricks, I could not move them. I didn't know what was happening to me. Then my arms were no longer moveable. I begged for God to help me. My eyes were getting blurrier by the moment causing me to lose my sight so rapidly that I could scarcely see at all. But yet far ahead of me, I was barely able to make out the forms of what I thought looked like my husband and two young daughters. It seemed like they were getting away…Oh thank God. I screamed in my heart, run, my husband, run with all your might. Run, my lovely daughters, run, and please, whatever you do, do not turn to look back. Oh how I longed more than anything to be with them at that moment, how I wished I could run along-side them. I would have been content to just walk, but I could not. I could not move, I could not even blink my eyes. I was secured solidly to the ground. And oh, that awful taste. There was a strong, overwhelming taste filling my throat and my mouth, it was choking me, I could not breathe. Then I realized what it was. It was salt, I could even smell it as it filled my nostrils, and it was all over me. Soon, my sight was completely gone, and my movements had been completely stilled. I would never walk again; neither would I ever again embrace my daughters. My husband would not ever feel the warmth of my body as we lay asleep at night. My hands could no longer prepare delicious meals for my family to enjoy. I wondered who would cook for them. Then my situation became clear to me as I realized my fate, I was destined to remain there in that very spot day and night for an eternity. Oh my God…what had I done, what had happened? I only wanted to remember what our city looked like when I turned back around. I thought one last glance would be sufficient. The Men of God told us to *"look not behind"* us or we would *"be consumed,"* but I didn't understand what that meant, I did not think one last look would matter. How was I to know that it would indeed be my last look, at anything?

Well, there I stood, not by the strength of my own power, but by the sheer force of this brick-like salt that had overtaken and consumed me. I had become a pillar of salt. I remained there for what seemed like thousands of years, unmovable and rooted in that one spot while the entire horrible scene of the day of the fire replayed itself in my awareness more times than I can recall. And although I could neither see nor hear, I was somehow keenly aware of the passing of time, and of my presence on the pages of the history of humankind. From what I understand, the story of the fierce destruction of Sodom and Gomorrah has become legendary and is retold many times over. The legend is a very detailed one, including even the strangers who visited us on the day of the fire, that they had also visited Uncle Abraham a few days earlier. I understand that the story also describes the uninvited visit from the men of our city of Sodom shortly after the strangers had arrived at our home. This amazing account was put in writing and placed in a chronicle of births, lives, deaths and events dating as far back as Father Adam. The writer I am told was a man whose name was Moses, a descendant of Uncle Abraham. Quite the writer, his account has captured the attention of people for millennia as they held a fascination about the one last thing I did that day which caused me to remain rooted right where I stood. It has been a popular fascination that provided much food for discussion and speculation about me. Long after my husband, my daughters, my grandchildren and multiple generations of my family have lived and died my reputation has loomed as an infamous monument to my one last act.

While I cannot challenge Moses' details of the story, even to his highlighting of my unfortunate end, I can declare it does not capture the essence of who I was, how I lived and what I felt on the day of the fire. You see, my life was quite full and very busy before the city in which I lived was destroyed. So, if you please, I would like to tell my account of what happened on that fateful day, the day of the fire.

I am Lot's wife. Your history writings do not identify me by my name, nor has anyone taken the time to inquire of my name, not even Moses. Instead, everyone down through the years has simply chosen to identify me as Lot's wife. But, I had a name, it was the name my father gave me, and I loved it. I loved it especially when Lot spoke my name the day he asked permission of my father to take me as his wife. How I wish you too had known my name, I think you would have liked it.

Lot and I moved to Sodom after his uncle Abraham decided to separate his herds from ours. He said the one family with all of its animals and servants, was too large to manage effectively, and that our servants were always arguing with his servants. So, based on Uncle Abraham's decision, my husband Lot could no longer dwell with his cousins and other family members, but had to go in another direction and away from his beloved uncle. Lot was very grieved by that decision, because he loved his Uncle Abraham so very much. Uncle Abraham had been more like a father to my husband, since Lot's own father died in the early days of Lot's youth, and Uncle Abraham had raised Lot into his adult years. They both cried on the day of their parting, not wanting to separate themselves from each other; but the dissention between the servants and herdsmen, and the need for more land for each of them, forced the matter. Because Uncle Abraham loved Lot so, he gave Lot first choice about which direction he wanted to go. My husband looked around at the land stretching before us, and made his decision to go toward Sodom. And so we went.

After arriving in Sodom, I was intrigued by the amount of activity going on in that city. People in large numbers were always going somewhere or coming from another. All the fast-paced movement took some getting used to. It was so very different from the slower and more deliberate pace of life on the plains and in the deserts. But before long, we settled in to life in Sodom. And despite the different lifestyle of the Sodomites, my husband, my girls, and I made friends among our neighbors, and the populace of the city.

Amid the people I befriended and who befriended us, I had two especially close friends, Milahah, and Suphenah. The three of us did many things together and visited each other often. We shopped and bargained, planted, cooked and lived life as best we knew how. It was routine for us to purchase beautiful, colored cloths from the merchants and make lovely garments of elaborate design for our children and husbands. We compared the sizes of the fruit and vegetables we had grown, each declaring our own to be larger and riper than the others. We insisted that our own animals were bigger and stronger than anyone else's. We laughed and giggled, and sometimes cried together as we shared our stories about our husbands and our lives under their control.

One day two strangers came to visit my family with some disturbing news. They told us we had to leave Sodom very quickly and come with them because God was going to destroy both Sodom and Gomorrah. The news of our guests must have spread rapidly, because soon after their arrival, the men of Sodom came to the house wanting to visit with the strangers. My husband Lot refused to allow the men of Sodom into the house and offered our daughters out to them instead. I always hated it when things like that happened. But despite how I felt, I knew that women and girls were of little value to society for anything other than breeding, working, and satisfying the sexual desires of men. Everything inside me felt like a clump of dough being kneaded for baking, whenever I heard a man speak like that of a woman. And now, my precious daughters were being bargained without a second thought as substitutes and replacements for what the men of Sodom really wanted, the two men visiting our home. Possessing no authority to protect my babies or even object to their usury, I cried within. Let them have the strangers if they want them, I moaned in silence, just leave my girls alone.

Thus I was so very thankful when the strangers did not allow Lot to exchange our daughters for themselves. I was also intrigued by their power when they put a stop to the madness outside our door by blinding the men of the city who seemed determined to break down our door. Then in the midst of the mayhem, the strangers began rushing us out of our house and hurrying us along the streets towards the desert and out of the city.

Surrounded by all of the rushing and immediate decision making, I couldn't help but feel – please God forgive me – a little bit of pride as my two older daughters and their husbands refused to be influenced by the admonishing words of the aggressive strangers telling us to quickly leave the city. They made their own decisions to remain in Sodom but we had our two younger daughters with us. But now…how I wish they had come with us. I die over and over again whenever I think of what happened to them in Sodom. In my mind, I can still see them standing in the door of our house, watching us being rushed away by the strangers. Oh God, I hope they did not suffer. And what of my friends Milahah and Suphenah? My last memory of them is seeing them amongst the crowd outside our house, inquiring with their eyes, and searching mine for answers; where was I going, and why was I leaving in such a hurry, and why had I not told them good-by. I had no answers then, and I have none now. The two strangers possessed such strength, as they rushed us out of Sodom and away into the desert. Then, as unexpectedly as they had arrived at our house, they just as quickly disappeared once we reached the border of the city. All we heard were their parting words, *"Look not behind you."* That is when I made my fatal mistake. I took that last look, having no idea it would indeed be my last look at anything, nor that I would end up as I did, a pillar of salt.

My husband and younger daughters made it to safety. But, as happy as I am that they escaped the fate I endured, I am saddened by what happened in that cave between them. My daughters had not been given the opportunity to study under the tutelage of the great scholars of Sodom. My husband felt it to be an unforgivable waste of time, effort, and money to educate a woman in subjects other than basket weaving, herding, cooking, sewing, and the like. Therefore, he left whatever learning they would acquire completely in my charge. Thus, Milahah and Suphenah became like second mothers to my daughters, as I also became to Milahah and Suphenah's daughters. And so, while I am happy about my daughter's escapes, I grieve about what happened in the cave between them and their father. I am brokenhearted to know that Lot my husband, lay with our girls, his own daughters. Having not lived anywhere other than Sodom, my daughters thought Sodom was all there was to the world. Their ignorance told them that no other cities or countries existed now that Sodom and Gomorrah had been destroyed. In their lack of knowledge, they thought they would never marry, and that it was their responsibility to keep the population of mankind from dying in the cave with them. So, since they thought no other men were available to make this happen, they devised a plan of procreation, with their father being the vehicle for propagation. They gave their father enough wine to drink causing him to be unaware that the pleasure of lying with a woman was being derived from knowing his own daughters. But how could Lot have been that drunk? How could he not have known? They were his daughters, could he not have recognized their voices, their smells? Perhaps because he had spent precious little time with them as they were growing up to recognize anything about them, he thought it was just the pleasure of a woman he was enjoying. I wonder if in his drunken state he thought it was me?

Well, much time passed while I stood there in that very same spot millennia after millennia, pondering so many things in my awareness, having so many regrets, and experiencing so many emotions, most of which were sad and grievous. The people of the country where I was frozen in time have grown so accustomed to my presence that they introduce me, or what remains of me, as a tourist attraction. Tourists photograph me and speculate about whether that salt/stone figure is really me, the same Lot's wife of Biblical history. Still others simply dismiss me as a unique rock formation brought about by the influences of nature's elements, and centuries of weather changes.

But one day, something quite miraculous and wonderful happened. During one of my never ending moments of depression and overwhelming grief, I heard a voice, a most comforting, and soothing voice. It spoke directly to me, yet was not coming from a distant place outside of me, but seemed to emanate from within me, from right inside the

44

thick layers of rock-like salt where I resided. The voice did not refer to me as Lot's wife, but greeted me by my very own name and said, "I love you."

Oh Dear God in heaven, what was this I was hearing? No one has ever said those words to me. Not even Lot had ever told me he loved me. I was utterly confused, yet for the first time since the day of the fire, I felt warmed inside. I wanted to hear those words again, and again. And then, from within the cold, rock salt existence that I was, I heard them again; "I love you." The voice very gently and lovingly became tangible and visible. The voice became revealed as the one whose name is Jesus. He said He was the Son of God sent into the world to redeem it, to actually redeem everyone who had ever and would ever live in this world. He said He had just been crucified, having completed the ultimate assignment that He and His Father many generations ago had determined would be necessary. He had left His human body in a tomb and was with me fulfilling another portion of His mission. I felt so embraced and for the first time, safe. He said He would be spending the next three days releasing captives and freeing bound souls. But sensing my anxiety at being separated from Him, He told me that while He was elsewhere doing that, I would still have His undivided attention and would continue to feel His complete presence. How could He possibly see about the needs of so many others and yet remain with me, I pondered? Selfishly, I concluded I did not care, as long as He kept His promise to be with me.

Those were the best three days of my life, human or stone. We had long conversations while He was with me. He told me He forgave my disobedience in looking back at Sodom, that He knew I had paid dearly for it. He assured me my daughters who had lain with Lot were OK and that they had been responsible for the establishment of two very great nations, the Moabites and the Ammonites. They each gave birth to a son. My eldest daughter named her son Moab, and my youngest daughter named her son Ben Ammi. Jesus also said He would be seeing my two best friends, Milahah and Suphenah within the three-day period, and not to worry about them because He was going to make things alright with them as well. When He told me He loved them too, I didn't feel slighted, nor did I feel His love for me diminished in any way. I felt no competition for His love for me. In fact, I somehow knew the love He had for me would never fade. He also assured me that my two older daughters and their husbands would also benefit from His three-day visitation to the world of the dead. He just kept telling me such wonderful things about how all the people who had ever done anything wrong would be given the opportunity for forgiveness. He mentioned He was having a Celebration of Freedom, for the releasing of shackles and fetters that held so many bound, and that He was even going to pay a visit to Father Adam, and his son Cain and was going to forgive Cain for murdering his brother Abel.

It has been several millennia since the wonderful visit from Jesus; I can still feel His presence. I never shall forget as I continue to bask in the memories of the three days we spent together. That rock solid pillar of salt that comprised me, continued to experience the warmth Jesus brought to me. I never again felt the constant, agonizing pain I knew before His visit, nor was I tortured by the continuous changes in weather conditions. I did not feel depressed anymore because I lived in excited anticipation of His return. He told me He was returning to get everyone who believed in Him as Savior of the world. That upon His return, He would not leave me behind as in His first visit but would take me back with Him along with all the others. I would live with Him, where my identity would no longer be just Lot's wife. His plan was to give me a new name, and praise God, a new body. So, whenever anyone visits the Hashemite Kingdom of Jordan, and sees me standing in solitude, high upon the rocky cliffs, overlooking the foamy shores of the Salt Sea, which is now known as the Dead Sea, if they look closely, they might see the smile on my face because I know Jesus is coming back, and I wait patiently until His return. And by the way Jennifer, when you write our stories I would love it if you would place a photo of me on the cover of your book about us.

Chapter 4
For Sale by Owner

Rahab began to speak. Her voice was soft but she spoke without apology and her projection was confident. My name is Rahab and I held membership in a worldwide society. Some call it the oldest profession known to humanity, others call it an undesirable lifestyle, others a means to an end, and still others an unavoidable component of survival. Known by many names, its definition changes based upon who is defining it. Language in Jennifer's 21st century defines this profession as prostitution, while the language of ancient biblical texts defines people in this profession as harlots. But by whichever name one chooses to define prostitution, it is successful only when the parties involved cooperate with each other. It goes without saying that the reasons for cooperation between prostitutes/harlots and those who purchase their services, are as complex as the matter is itself; availing ones sexual abilities and favors to another for a monetary, mutually agreed upon compensation.

With this as a backdrop, we can look into biblical history and see my name, Rahab. My name is identified as belonging to the woman best known as the most prominent prostitute of biblical literature. Scripture uses the word harlot. And while I was known primarily as a harlot, there was so much more to me than has ever been told. Once a child like everyone else in human society, I at one point in life was a young woman budding into full womanhood, with a family, a mother a father, and siblings. And while some documentation even identifies me as an entrepreneurial seller of purple, I am still most remembered for my participation in the world of practicing harlots. Yet, there was so very much more to me than that. As an astute business woman, I recognized at a young age that I possessed a commodity men loved and craved, and were willing to pay for. I seized the moment time and time again, supplying them with the services for which they hungered and never seemed to be satisfied. This provided me a way to sustain myself, earn a decent living, and create a fairly comfortable lifestyle for myself and my family.

But because my story was written by another, without my input, I have traveled forward in time to tell my own story as I lived it. Being the subject of this tale, I have come here into your time Jennifer, into this 21st century to bring clarity and understanding about my life, straight from my own experience.

I was born into a poor family. My father was not one of the leaders of the community, he wasn't sought-after for wisdom and advice, nor was he one of the ones who sat by the gate with the elders discussing important issues of the times. He too had been born into a very poor family and had simply acquiesced to the hand of deprived existence that providence had so unfairly dealt him. Poverty was all he had ever known, and while it was a sad and unfortunate way of life, it held for him a strange comfort, in that it was familiar. Thus, when he desired a wife, it was clear that his selection for a mate could only be made from a pool of people living in conditions of similar lifestyles. Even with the birth of each of his children, the only legacy he could pass on to them was what he knew like the back of his hand, scarcity and lack. His ability to provide the basic necessities of food, shelter and clothing for his family was severely compromised. And so it was that inadequacy not only thrived in his household, but multiplied ad infinitum, and insufficiency prospered without restraint. He had four sons and four daughters, and I Rahab, was his middle child. From the moment I began to talk, I was the one who constantly asked questions, always seeming to need explanations for everything. I was a source of exasperation to my parents and annoyed my poor siblings with never ending questions and demands for the right answers, instead of the empty, meaningless ones I usually received. I wasn't easily satisfied because I refused to be placated, or pacified; I wanted honest responses, but alas, I seldom received them. Whenever I perceived the response to one of my queries to be an attempt at appeasement rather than the complete truth, I would leave the conversation disappointed, frustrated, and often annoyed. I struggled within my young world of reasoning to understand why adults persisted in being less than truthful. Their answers always left me feeling empty. But the consistently unanswered, perplexing, and most painful question, was why it was necessary for us to remain hungry day after day after day. At a very young age I observed there was an abundance of food in the markets, and in the fields, and among the traveling merchants, so why wasn't more of it available for my family. Sadly, my father's explanations were never quite satisfactory.

By the age of about eight years old, I had developed quite a keen mind and a strong sense of survival. I felt somehow challenged to find a way to make my life less painful and more comfortable. My primary obsession became focused on one thing, to somehow find a way to live without being in a state of constant hunger. It pained me to see my younger siblings spending their entire days searching for food, while my older siblings acted as if they were indifferent to our lack of it. I knew better, I knew they really were hungry. My mother scavenged everywhere she could to gather scraps from wherever she found them to prepare meals for us. My father tried desperately to maintain a semblance of pride while he did what he could to either bring food or money into the household. And on those few and rare occasions when we enjoyed a fairly decent meal, it was the same to us as if we were feasting at a banquet. My strength of mind concluded that something had to be done whatever and wherever that something was, it had to be done. So I resolved to be the one to discover the something that would change my life for the better, particularly since no one else in my family had done so.

Gradually my patterns of behavior began to change. Having always been the observant one in the family, the one always asking "why?" my incessant questioning was slowly diminishing as I grew older. Developing afresh in its place was a more casual and less inquisitive personality. Without sounding immodest, I admit that a delightful and infectious new me was emerging accompanied by a new, quick-witted imaginative manner of speaking. My new charm made people laugh and engaged them in relaxed conversation; especially the men. I had found my place, perhaps even the *something* for which I had been searching. I was experiencing a side of life not previously known to me, a sense of having my own power.

It felt really good to possess this power, so I put aside and disregarded one of the very main traditions within my culture, the one which forbade single, unmarried women from open casualness in the presence of men and blatant public interaction with them. But I was unwilling to let go of the awareness that I now possessed a new kind of influence, especially with men, so I clung fiercely to my newly acquired gift. And I felt especially justified when on few occasions, a grateful man feeling particularly generous, would reciprocate my attention with a loaf of bread, and sometimes even a coin. I immediately recognized the far reaching implications of the potentially monetary outcome of my newly acquired skill. The gratefulness of the men was transformed into tangible rewards, and I quickly realized I could not leave such opportunities solely to chance. If I were to benefit from my new found freedom, I knew I would have to create the moments myself. So I devised a plan.

I discovered a location to implement my plan. I selected a cool spot where the breezes were plentiful, under a huge shade tree at a crossroad along the prominent roadways leading in and out of the small village where I grew up, and into the surrounding larger cities. There I would stand as a one-woman welcoming committee for the men journeying along the way. Some were returning home from their arduous day in the fields, some were shepherds, some were traveling merchants, and still others were simply out and about, looking for adventure. As they passed by, I would flash my lovely smile, express a brief greeting, or otherwise engage them in conversation. I would sometimes challenge them with a humorous riddle.

It wasn't long before the men desired more from me than just greetings, smiles, and riddles; they wanted the more personal contact that was reserved for the marriage bed only. Therefore, based on their promises of what they would give me, I gave them what they desired; we were each giving and receiving. And although frowned upon by the people within my tiny village, this exchange became quite profitable for me, so I continued. My decision not only benefited my personal gains, but it also enhanced the lives of my family members as well. Because over a time the occasional loaf of bread became several consistent loaves, and one coin multiplied into many. My dear mother no longer needed to scrape and plead for morsels of food for her family. She walked through the market places with her basket picking and choosing the items she wanted. Begging soon became a memory of what used to be. And as painful and unpleasant as that reality had once been, it had now become just an old memory for her. Ignoring the glares of disapproval from the merchants as she paid for her food, my mother understood that while her money may have been obtained by less than honorable means, the merchants had no misgivings about accepting it from her. The whispers of the other women meant precious little to my mother when she compared her present state of comfort to her previous condition of desperate lack and borderline starvation.

My very proud father began to wear a look of dubious pride because he was no longer the object of village ridicule. His family was being well provided for; their garments were no longer the tattered clothes of the destitute. And while he still was not permitted to sit at the gate with the elders and men of distinction, he at least was no longer disregarded as the insignificant village beggar, and he clearly was not being ignored. The men of the village looked at him face to face; they ceased—as they once did—to stare right past him as though he did not exist. While he knew their thoughts about him and his inability to keep his daughter from doing what she did, his greatest joy came because finally he was no longer being looked away from, but rather eye-to-eye, man to man. For the first time in my life, I saw my father walk about through the village with his head up, nodding his head in acknowledgement to all who greeted him. As they encountered him along the roads, or glimpsed him from a distance, the men looked directly at my father and not away from him as before. If for no other reason than that alone, I was proud of what I was and what I was doing.

My new lifestyle allowed me to obtain many of the wonderful material things my youthful heart once longed for. After a time, I was able to purchase a more spacious home atop the wall that surrounded the near-by city, Jericho. There I lived in modest comfort with my family. Then one day they came; two men of the people of Israel whom I had never seen

56

before came directly to my house, saying they had come to Jericho to spy out the terrain. They were to take a report about Jericho back to their commander Joshua as to the vulnerability of our city and the strength of our army. The reputation of these men, their people and their God had already preceded them. Everyone in Jericho and surrounding cities had heard the stories of their power and might, and how their God had intervened for them on so many occasions. There was a genuine fear in the hearts of the warriors about those people of Israel and their strange and powerful God. We all hoped we would never have to encounter them for fear of complete destruction by their God.

But here they were, right in my house having not the slightest hesitation about telling us what their plans were for our city. The intention of their commander Joshua was to storm our city, destroy all life within it, burn everything to the ground and take the city for himself and his people. I wasn't quite sure why these Israelite men were being so forthright with me, but I saw an immediate opportunity for survival and proposed a cooperative alliance with them. I told them that since word had gotten out of their entrance into Jericho and were at my house, the King of Jericho had sent me word he was dispatching his best men to capture them and ordered me to cooperate in the capture. So, applying my most persuasive charm, I convinced the men of Israel that I would protect them from our King and arrange for their escape back to their camp if they would promise not to harm me nor my family when their commander Joshua returned with his army to destroy the city. They accepted my plan. I hid them on the roof of my house among my flax inventory and lied to the Kings soldiers when they arrived, telling them the men of Israel had taken flight to the hills when they heard of the King's search for them. I assured the soldiers they could easily overtake the spies if they hurried.

Then in keeping with the plan, I helped the men of Israel escape over the wall and away from the city after the King's men were gone. After that I hung my best and most expensive scarlet sash in my window as the agreed upon signal to the army of Israel that this house was to be spared when they returned to destroy Jericho.

Before long, the army of Israel returned and surrounded the outer side of the wall of our city. For six days we could hear their marching and movement around our city on the opposite side of the wall. What were they doing? Then on the seventh day, we heard a new sound. It was the sound of the blaring of their horns and the deafening shouts of men at war. I and my family members all huddled together in fear as our house shook violently because it was situated on the wall of the city, and the very wall itself was crumbling to the ground all around us. Steeped in fear, we remained hopeful that the two spies of Israel would be men of their word to spare us in this deadly attack. Amid the blinding and choking dust, the quaking of the earth, the chaos of battle, the piercing screams and lamenting cries from victims of slaughter, arose the desperate, paralyzing fear that we might have been betrayed. Perhaps they were not going to return for us and we were to be destroyed along with everyone else. Then we saw them. Emerging from the darkness of the dust came several men. It was impossible to recognize or even see their faces but we responded without hesitation as we felt them grabbing us and telling us to come with them. As we took flight from the city, I looked behind me to see what had become of our house. To my utter amazement, I saw our house standing like a single pillar of strength still atop a lone segment of the original wall that had once so completely and protectively surrounded the great city of Jericho. But now, the entire wall was gone, crumbled into mounds and heaps on the ground. There was nothing left standing except that one solitary section of wall which remained upright, in support of our house while everything else around it was gone. And in the dusty wind, I could still see my beautiful, bright scarlet sash drawing attention to itself as it billowed and snapped in the wind.

After the terrible battle, I was taken into that huge band of many, many people who called themselves Israelites. I had the opportunity to meet their fearless commander Joshua who seemed to thrive and draw strength from the never ending battles he fought. His love for fighting was so great that he sought out countries and foreign nations to attack and challenge into battle. His passion for fighting was second however only to the profound love and endless loyalty he felt and demonstrated toward his precious God of Israel.

My life began anew as my former profession ceased. I and my family were accepted by this huge group of people as though we belonged and had always been members of their vast community. The people of Israel were very religious with many rules and feasts and sacrifices in celebration of their fearful God, and I felt myself beginning to dearly love and respect them. Initially my emotions about these people confused me considering how much I had previously feared them and dreaded any mention of their name or their God. Yet after a time, one of these handsome Israelite men captured my heart and I loved him in a way I had not loved a man before. His name was Salmon and he asked my father for my hand in marriage. Salmon and I were married and had children and it was through our son Boaz that I became the mother-in-law to a lovely young widow named Ruth. Interestingly enough, Ruth had also been an outsider until she married my son and was received and embraced by the nation of Israel.

So, during my subsequent long and satisfied life as Salmon's wife and mother of many children, I learned by experience that this God was so much more than the terrible and fearful God of His reputation. Greater than any other deity I had ever heard of or worshipped, I found Him to be a most generous and loving God lavishing numerous wonderful benefits upon all those who loved Him and who abided by His statutes. Discovering that no other gods existed and that He was the only One, I embraced Him as my very own *God who forgives*. He and I developed a most endearing and passionate relationship with one another; I coveted the quiet times I was able to steal away alone with Him on the hillsides and meadows when no one else was around. And because He nurtured me so completely with an intimacy I had never known before, He became the love of my heart and the strength of my existence. For all of these life-changing reasons, I remember with a warm excitement, the day I determined in my heart that I would also be an Israelite woman.

It was many generations later, after I had passed into the Realm-of-Those-Who-Sleep, that I came face to face with the anticipated Messiah spoken of by my people. Introducing Himself as Jesus the Christ, He honored me one evening with a visit and the news that the children I bore had been direct ancestors of His human lineage. I wept in appreciation and could think of no grander honor than to have given birth to ancestors of the true and living Son of God. I, a former seller of my most private intimacies had been granted this unthinkable and undeserved privilege. Jesus the Christ speaking so gently, reminded me of the numerous sin and atonement sacrifices prepared by the ancient Israelites, said that because He had just given His human life as the ultimate and final sacrifice for every human issue and sin; no further sacrifices for time eternal would ever again be necessary.

I could scarcely believe what I was hearing. He explained further that His death had just taken place within the past two hours and for the next three days He would be spending time in the Realm-of-Those-Who-Sleep releasing captives and offering them freedom. We had such sweet and wonderful communion while He spoke and I felt so comforted by His presence, that I wanted Him to remain for the rest of time. I pleaded with Him to stay with me. He responded since there was much to do to complete His plan He could only stay with me for three days. But He assured me that even after the 3 days had passed, His presence would remain with me until He physically returned again. And on that next visit, He would take me and all others who abided in His will, back with Him to His place called Glory. I shall never forget His visit, and I wait with excited anticipation for His return.

Chapter 5
Twelve Pieces

He was a Levite. His duty as a Levite was to help in the service of the Temple of the LORD. Service of the Temple included managing the courtyards and side rooms, setting out the bread on the table, keeping inventory of the special flour for the grain offerings and the thin loaves made without yeast. Baking, mixing, and measuring for correct quantities and sizes were also among his duties. In addition, the purification of all sacred things landed on the list of tasks performed by the Levites.

And while he had many duties in his capacity as a Levite, clearly, the one that was his favorite and dearest to his heart, was assisting the Priests in the slaughtering of animals in preparation for the burnt sacrifices. He found a strange fascination and excitement in the process and ritual of it all. Thus, he became more adept at this line of duty than any of the other aspects of service to the Lord in the Temple. Slaughtering was his specialty and he was an expert at it. The smell of blood was a familiar aroma to his nostrils and his hands were often coated with the sticky consistency of old, drying blood. His nail-beds were dark from the stain of many layers of clotted blood. And beneath his nails, could be seen solid clumps of animal skin, fur, entrails, and dung. With casual expertise he could drain every drop of blood from an animal's body. It was with flawless precision that he would skin an animal, remove the internal organs of a beast, separate the head of a goat from the rest of its body, amputate the legs of a calf, or otherwise divide and sever with ease into many pieces of separate body parts from the whole. Cutting, bloodletting, chopping, and dissecting, were the most beloved of all the other elements of his trade; subsequently he sought these tasks as often as he could. Up to this point, his slaughtering activities had been restricted to animals being prepared for altar sacrifices. But this was about to change. Because soon, on a very eerie and unique occasion, it would be a human person, a woman, upon whom he would impose his carving expertise.

That woman was a pitiful, unfortunate woman who found herself helpless to provide her own defense against his dismembering practices. The world in which she lived offered her almost no recourse of action against assault or harm exacted upon her by her husband. Her own society denied her the very protection of human rights owed to all people. In fact, this ruthless society granted permission for her to be hopelessly captive and helplessly trapped in this man's life while he treated her with whatever disregard his whims or distorted logic dictated at any given moment. Without apology, this world in which they both lived made not the slightest suggestion of restraint to this man who with meticulous intent literally destroyed this defenseless woman, limb by limb, and piece by piece. I am that woman, but my name is not written in our sacred literature.

The day was scorching hot. The sweltering heat was influenced by the season of the year, but most especially by the position of the high, noon-day sun, beaming directly down from over-head. The forcefulness of the sun's rays were unforgiving in their aim. Every day, while in this exact mid-day placement in the sky, the sun, for this brief period of time allowed no respite from the precision of its glare. It permitted no formation of shade for comfort or cooling. During this kind of weather, particularly during this time of day, most people sought the shelter of their tents or the protection of their homes. But now, fearing for my safety I was frightened, desperate and battered, and despite the heat of the day, there I was trudging wearily, stumbling, almost crawling, along the hot, dusty roads. I was on my way to my father's house.

It had only been a few short months ago that a Levite had taken me as his concubine from my father's house. And life with the Levite had proven not to be a good life. It was not at all what I had hoped it would be. He was cruel, he was demanding, and he showed me neither passion nor compassion. Life with him had been completely void of even a hint of kindness. Therefore, I unwittingly found myself accepting what I thought was love, from other men. They demonstrated the kind of care I so desperately hoped would have come from my husband. Somehow I knew my behavior was wrong, yet it felt so good. It wasn't very long before my mounting feelings of guilt, my anger toward my husband for not providing me with sufficient affection to have kept me from seeking it in the arms of others—although I alone bear the burdensome blame for abandoning my marriage vows—and finally my fear of more beatings from my husband when he discovered my unfaithfulness, all forced me to make a decision I never thought I would. I had to leave the home I shared with my husband and return to my father's house. After all, my father's house had been the only place in my life that had been safe. Therefore, putting aside all concern for appearances, I found myself after so short a time, returning back to the home of my father. What an embarrassment, what a shameful admission that I had been unsuccessful as a wife. Yet, even though viewed as a sign of failure and an open declaration of disgrace, still, I came back to my father's house. Humiliation notwithstanding, I knew there would be no beatings in my father's house, only safety there. I knew my mother and sisters would welcome me back. They did. But they cried when they first saw me as they surrounded and comforted me and brought me into the house. With salves made from healing spices and oils, they tended to the bruises on my back, arms and thighs. They applied ointments and herbs to the open wounds on my face, scalp, and breasts. With sun bleached linen, soaked in special compounds, they wrapped the bare scalp on my head where clumps of hair had been violently ripped out by the roots. They took turns prodding me to eat, encouraging me to gain back my strength. They sat with me while I slept, reassuring me back to sleep when I woke myself with my own piercing screams from frightful nightmares. I remained there for four months, recovering from my painful bruises and deeply inflicted cuts, recovering under the tender care of my mother and sisters. The patches of bare scalp on my head began to disappear underneath the re-growth of soft, new hair.

But all too soon, the nightmare that everyone feared the most became a dreadful reality. My husband the Levite came to get me. During the entire time prior to his coming, no one had asked for an explanation of my battered condition upon my return home, and I had not offered one. There had been no whispered sharing of secrets, and no searching for information. But the Levite was back to get me, and there were no customs or laws granting me protection from him or the right to refuse him. I was his property.

My father extended the customary courtesy one offers to visitors. He entreated his daughter's husband to stay and eat with the family, to wait awhile, and not take his leave until the morning. My husband consented. Morning came and my father convinced his son-in-law to remain yet another day. After several days of convincing, the Levite would be persuaded no more, he would fulfill his purpose in coming. He took me and left. Not ever before had my father seen such a look of dreaded fear on my face as I gave my family a final pleading glance, then walked slowly away with tentative steps, behind my husband. My father couldn't bear to follow with his eyes the sight of his terrified daughter as I gradually disappeared across the burning sand walking several paces behind my husband and his servant.

After several days of travel and too few rest stops, the Levite found himself in the city of Gibeah, accepting the invitation for overnight lodging in the home of a stranger. The stranger, a gracious host, was hospitable in that he provided the Levite and his company the opportunity to refresh themselves. Then came a sumptuous meal and a time of relaxed conversation between our host, my husband and his servant. At about dusk, the relaxation was interrupted by a forceful banging on the door by a group of rowdy young men demanding to be introduced to the Levite and his male servant. The host knew full well that an introduction was least on the minds of the men at the door, so he offered his daughter instead. He gave the men his permission to do whatever they pleased with her. The men refused his offer. And by this time, the Levite had become exasperated with all the fuss; he wanted to get back to the relaxation of the evening. So with this he grabbed my arm and pulled me to the door, sternly instructed the young men to take me and do whatever they needed to, but by all means leave him, his host and his male servant alone to enjoy what was left of the evening.

Reluctantly, the men accepted me but they were angry because their original demands had not been honored. So they appeased their anger by imposing as many despicable, and sordid sexual acts upon me that their evil minds could conceive. They were abusive and punitive in what they did to me and forced me to do. All the while they forbade me to scream or cry out. The horror lasted the entire night until finally at dawn, they became exhausted and went their way, leaving me lying battered on the ground, face down in their fluids and my own blood. With what minimal strength I had remaining, I made my way back to the home of the hospitable stranger who had opened his doors to us. I knew I needed to keep the Levite from having to come and find me. It would have greatly displeased him if he had had to search for me. Barely making it back to the house, I collapsed right at the outside of the door, my arms outstretched, and my hands clutching onto the threshold of the door.

It was now well into the daylight of the early morning hours and the Levite, having enjoyed a restful night's sleep, and eager to continue his journey, prepared to leave the hospitality of the generous stranger. As he bade the stranger good-by and left the house, he stumbled over me, a helpless heap of a bloodied, beaten woman lying on the ground at the door. As I lay there semi-conscious, he stepped over me and ordered me to get up and make myself ready to leave with him. I did not move, nor did I respond. Why was I not responding to his demands and why was I publicly disrespecting him so openly? Annoyed at having to begin his day with an unresponsive woman, and not wishing to continue the public display of blatant disrespect, he picked me up, slung me over his donkey as if I were a mere carcass and began his journey home. But I do not know if I even had the strength to have responded. I was barely alive and had lost too much blood to respond. I felt myself lapsing into a state of unconsciousness. Was I dead? Even I could not tell. By the time we reached home, I had not become responsive or spoken one word to the Levite during the entire journey. My silence it seemed to him, was an indication that I was a very obstinate and stubborn woman. This would not be tolerated. So, still raging from everything that had previously occurred, and especially now with this new disrespectful behavior, he began the grisly task he had decided must be done. I wanted to scream out in horrific pain when I felt the first agonizing and piercing deep cut across the back of my left shoulder, but I did not have the strength to scream. After that, everything went black, I felt nothing more. Instead, I seemed to be standing outside myself watching my husband complete his gruesome undertaking. He very carefully and precisely with the same tools he used on animal sacrifices, but now sharpened for this occasion, divided me limb from limb, and cut my body into 12 pieces. He then sent each dismembered part of my body to a different location within the collective coasts and borders of Israel's people.

Nothing like this had ever been done before among the people of Israel. Never before, from this very moment, nor as far back as the exodus out of Egypt, had Israel's lineage experienced anything like this. Never! So when the Israelite leaders of the cities of Dan, Beersheba and Gilead confronted my husband to inquire about how such a terrible thing as this could have happened, he simply told them that the men of Gibeah had come after him to kill him, but instead they raped me. My husband acknowledged that after he had been so disgraced by my rape, he cut my body into twelve pieces and because the lewd atrocities had taken place in Israel, he felt obliged to send a part of my body to each region of Israel's inheritance. Not one time did my husband take responsibility for what had occurred by telling the Dan, Beersheba and Gilead leaders that he himself had sent me out to the men for them to do with me as they pleased. Not once did my husband ever express sadness for my painful and humiliating experiences at the hands of those men. Not once did he ever speak remorse for the abominable outcome after we returned home. And in addition, not once did the leaders of Israel acknowledge my husband's wrongdoing or improper conduct in the entire episode.

Well, much time progressed, many, many centuries passed and the painful ache within the heart of my severed self still cried out for the rest of my lost self. Even though long dead with my body fragments scattered to places unknown, the anguish of my heart was still deeply felt by my

71

separated and unconnected self. But then one morning in the quiet stillness of the early breaking of day, amidst the usually nagging, tortured isolation of my dissected body, something amazing happened. A great and mighty presence emerged. It was a presence more powerful and commanding than anything that ever was, yet, unmistakably the most tranquil and comforting of all things ever. This awesome, gentle presence spoke so lovingly and softly to me that immediately from wherever they had all been, each segment of my body returned from their distant places, joined themselves together and became simultaneously whole again. My heart leaped with joy, my head turned as my eyes searched for the origin of this soothing presence that had encircled me. My arms reached out to embrace it. All of my members were reunited and functioning in tandem. No longer were they detached, but they were once again connected, un-bruised and un-battered. It was all too wonderful. Not even in life had I ever felt this way before. For the first time in my existence, I felt worthwhile. It seemed as though I had been totally forgiven of every past indiscretion. I had been cleansed. Suddenly, there was no reason for guilt, no space for shame. And while these feelings were so completely unfamiliar, they all felt so very right. Then amazingly and miraculously, the presence became visible and told me His name. "*I am Jesus.*" He told me He was the one who had just put me back together again, He had re-membered me and made me whole as an act of love. This most beautiful man who stood before me with such power and kindness, whose mere presence made me feel so safely protected, was now declaring His absolute love for me. His love however, felt quite different from all the other feelings I had mistakenly thought were love. His love was clean, it was pure, it was safe, it was genuine, and it comforted me in ways none of my other past experiences had ever done. He told me He loved me right now, had always loved me, would forever love me, and had come here now,

72

just to tell me so. I could barely stand it. He explained that He was the Son of God, here on earth with a mission in progress. He had just completed what He called a redemptive act, an execution on an old, splintered, wooden, rugged cross. He had willfully and deliberately relinquished His life during this agonizing experience and had been buried in a borrowed tomb. His need for the tomb was temporary because His plan was to leave His body in the tomb for only three-days while He went about completing the rest of His mission. As such He was now in the process of completing the second part of His redemptive mission by visiting all those who had died and whose souls were now residing in the world-of-the-dead. He was going to have a special celebration that would release the captive souls which had been bound until now. In my entire life I had never known anyone with such magnificent and tender power. Yet, here He was, right here with me assuring me of His loving care, and calming my anxiety with promises to remain with me even while He completed His visit to the world-of-the-dead. How could He possibly do that, I pondered? And as though He heard my very thoughts, He said He could do it because of who He was. He said, "*I am able to do all that I choose to do.*" I felt immediate solace.

Therefore, because those were the most satisfying and fulfilling three days in the existence of this no longer unfortunate woman, my feelings of abandonment and abuse have been replaced with a deep abiding contentment, and an excited anticipation. My new excitement is now based upon the promise Jesus made to me of a return visit at a future time. And I am so deeply content because of the blessed assurance He gave me that at His second coming, I would be included in the numberless mass of people He was coming to claim, to take back to Heaven with Him, to live in the eternity of time. What an absolute blessing. I am content to wait for it.

Chapter 6
My Baby Brother

Miriam spoke next. With a most loving smile on her face, she began to share her memories which she said were still very clear in her mind despite the centuries that had come and gone since the time of her experiences. She began speaking in a very clear and confident manner.

I can remember everything my mother said as clearly as if it were just yesterday, when she was with child with my youngest brother. I was the younger of my parent's two children, my brother Aaron and myself. We two were wide eyed with anticipation at the prospect of having another young one in the house among us but our parents didn't seem to share our excitement. There were pervading feelings of much uncertainty and anxiety in our home during those months. As the time drew closer for our mother to give birth to this much awaited child, the tension in our home became almost unbearable and thoughts once unheard of were now the primary wishes of my parents. It was understood that the value of a girl child was less than that of a strong healthy goat, yet my parents now found themselves wishing for a girl instead of a priceless and treasured male child. At this point in time they would gladly have satisfied themselves with the birth of a worthless girl into the family. You see, Pharaoh had issued a malevolent edict to kill every male newborn of every Hebrew woman. And in his maniacal state of determination, he had commanded even the Hebrew midwives to participate in this ghastly ruling by killing the innocent male infants as soon as each one was delivered. It was for this reason that our entire community was living in a constant state of fearful anguish and terror. Yet despite Pharaoh's murderous decree, the Hebrew midwives, at the risk of their own lives, acted heroically by disobeying Pharaoh's order because they loved their own Hebrew people and feared God much more than they feared Pharaoh.

Consequently, it was at their every opportunity that the Hebrew midwives permitted the Hebrew male infants to live. It was Shiphrah and Puah who became known as the two main Hebrew midwives who acted with such daring and gallant resistance. Turning to Jennifer, Miriam said, Jennifer dear, I believe you would call such action civil disobedience in your century. But even in the face of the brave efforts of these and other caring midwives, still some families had not experienced these benefits, but instead were living in broken-hearted devastation because a new-born male child born to them had already been slaughtered by the ruthlessness of Pharaoh's wicked and evil decree. Therefore, by the time our mother was at the point of near birth of her child, our entire family was at our wits end with fear. But we were relieved and rejoiced in God's timing when Puah arrived at our house to assist my mother in the birth.

And although Puah was successful in bringing my mother through her delivery process of this most precious infant who was indeed a beautiful baby boy, my mother was still beside herself with grief. Would Pharaoh's soldiers visit our home in search of a male newborn? Mother was delirious to the point of deep depression because of the possible fate that awaited her son. And although we were each straining against our own grief, we tried to console her, but she was inconsolable at the thought of her son's potentially brief life. According to Pharaoh, our baby boy's life would culminate at the end of an unforgiving, sharp edge of an Egyptian soldier's sword. This painful knowledge was known by Puah who tried to comfort us with her assurance that she would not report the birth, but her promise did not lessen our fear.

We each tried to console my mother, but we were of little help. However, something very strange began to fill the atmosphere in our house. Somehow we knew this baby was indeed no ordinary child and we believed that in some unknown way Pharaoh's edict would not interrupt the life of this new little one who had just come into our family, had captured our hearts and caused us to immediately love him so very much. We knew that despite our sense of powerlessness to rise against Pharaoh's order and our knowledge that we held no authority to overturn his proclamation, we also knew we could not stand helplessly by and cooperate with his command to execute the youngest and tiniest member of our small family. As the cycle of days becoming nights continued to repeat itself without a soldier's pounding at our door, there was a sense within us that the God we loved would remain protective. We somehow felt that in His lovingkindness to our family He would make it possible for our baby's life to be spared.

It had been a full three months, and we had been able to hide him right after his birth and keep him hidden for this entire time. Yet as time passed we knew another plan was needed to keep him safe. We reasoned that hiding him somewhere away from our house seemed our only option but we didn't know where that location would be. Where could we possibly hide him in order to keep him from being discovered? Then my mother came up with the idea of hiding him along the banks of the Nile River and it would be my duty to watch him and make sure he didn't drift afar into the deep or downstream into a neighboring city and out of our range of safety. I don't think we even considered how long we would be able to manage this hiding place, but we knew we had to at least begin with this plan. So, my father crafted a little cradle-boat and lined it with tar to keep the water out so baby would remain dry. My mother lined the basket with smooth hand-woven cloths and soft cushions. Then very early the next morning she lovingly placed my brother inside, and we walked to the banks of the Nile to put baby into the water inside his protective little boat. Mother and I slid off the river bank and stood for quite some time in the shallow water clinging to each other with the little basket between us knowing that this new plan could be a long and tiresome task. Finally, mother had to return home while I remained at the river with little brother. As I waded in the waist-deep water alongside my little brother, I sang psalms and lullabies to him as the gentle movement of the water tenderly rocked his little basket. I felt very protective of him during those morning and early afternoon hours and decided I would remain with him as long as I needed to even into and through the dark of the night. Each night I would pull his basket out of the water onto the edge of the river bank. I would take baby brother out of his cradle and into my arms, wrap us both in the warm and air-tight clock that mother had made for us. And there we would sleep until we were awakened by our mother in the early darkness of the next morning before the first breaking of the dawn. She would bring us a full days' worth of warm, freshly prepared food. And it was during those early morning moments that she would take advantage of the time and opportunity to lovingly nurse and caress her newborn son all the while covering him with kisses and speaking to him of his future greatness. Then she would exchange the previous day's cloths and blankets of his cradle with newly washed and sun-dried blankets and cloths which had also been fragranced with spices and herbs. Giving me my days' supply of fresh dry clothing, she encouraged me to begin my new day of watchful care. She would tell us both how much she loved us, carefully nestle baby brother back into his cradle and help me slip gently back into the water to begin yet another day of protective guard over our precious little one whom we were determined would not succumb to the slaughtering demise of Pharaoh's decree. Then quietly and quickly, mother would disappear into the darkness which soon gave way to the early light of the dawning new day.

Then one morning I saw her, she was beautiful. Her smooth and lovely, dark-brown skin glistened in the sunlight as she lowered herself into the Nile for her bath. It soon became clear to me that I was in the presence of royalty. I was nearly face-to-face with Pharaoh's daughter. How could someone so beautiful and so lovely be related in the remotest way to the hateful Pharaoh who declared that innocent newborn babies should be mercilessly executed before they had the slightest chance of living or breathing? But nonetheless, there she was, the beautiful daughter of Pharaoh. In my effort to conceal my presence by ducking under water and keeping hold of baby's cradle from beneath the water, I was not successful in keeping her from spotting the cradle. Before I realized what was happening, I could feel the tugging of the cradle by a pair of unknown hands. And for some reason, I felt safe in letting go. While still under water I swam to the nearest thicket of reeds to remain out of sight so I could lift my head above the water to breathe and see what had become of my baby brother whose crying I could hear from my short distance away. What I saw completely relieved me. Pharaoh's daughter along with her hand-maidens were smiling and cooing at baby brother attempting to comfort him from his crying and speaking softly to each other about how wonderful it was to find such a precious and delightful treasure within the waters of the Nile. Pharaoh's daughter then lifted him out of his cradle and held him ever so gently to her bosom and said, "This must be one of the Hebrew babies who has escaped my father's decree of death. It must be the will of the gods that his life has been spared so I would find him here floating in the waters of the Nile. And because I drew him out of the water, I will call his name Moses." She then gave a stern glare to

81

her hand-maidens and forbade them from ever revealing the circumstances of this infant Hebrew male, and further commanded that they keep in strictest secrecy even to their death this entire matter. She didn't stop there, but severely admonished them that their own death would be swift and immediate if so much as a whisper of the identity of this infant was ever divulged from their lips. And while my hopes for my brother's safety were lifted and encouraged, I nonetheless caught a glimpse of her father's ruthlessness in the formidable intensity with which his daughter by her stern posture on the matter brought absolute clarity of intent to her hand-maidens.

My hopes for my brother's safety were at once restored. Based on what I had just witnessed, I felt my strength returning, I was encouraged. I knew at that instance that my baby brother would be permitted to live, that he would be properly and lovingly cared for. And with that sense of renewed vigor, I emerged out from the shadows of the rustling reeds along the Nile river-banks and made myself known. I was sure there was no longer a need to hide, I could be safely visible. I had been encouraged by what I had just witnessed and my courage was strengthened. I approached Pharaoh's daughter ever so gently so as not to appear too forward or disrespectful in the presence of her royal distinction. "Who are you?" she asked me. And despite her question, I sensed that she somehow knew my presence there at the waters of the Nile was not simply a chance appearance at the exact moment she discovered a Hebrew newborn infant floating alone in the river neatly tucked in his tiny basket. I managed to find my voice and respond by offering not only my name but proposing a unique arrangement for the care of the child. "I can find a nurse from among the Hebrew women to care for the child if it would please you for me to do so." Her Royal Princess, Daughter of Pharaoh agreed and instructed me to go quickly and find such a woman and return with her to the palace immediately. I could barely believe my ears as my heart nearly burst with joy and excitement. "Yes, Your Royal Princess, Daughter of Pharaoh, I shall return quickly with such a woman." Then, I ran as fast as I could run arriving at our home almost completely out of breath and spouting out in breathless spurts the unbelievably good news to my mother. "I dare not believe such a wonderful report," my mother said. But just as quickly she added, "Yet I know that only our God can do such impossible things as you are telling me my child. Come, let us go back in haste to Pharaoh's Daughter and reclaim the child that the Lord has granted us." Once having arrived back at Pharaoh's Daughter's beautifully designated royal suite of rooms at the palace, my mother and I didn't want to appear too anxious for fear of her possible change of heart. After all, I had witnessed her harsh and severe demeanor when she forbade her handmaidens under penalty of death from revealing the identity of the infant; and I didn't ever want to see that side of her again. She told my mother to take the child and nurse him well and return him to the palace when he had been weaned. She said further that she would provide wages for my mother to do so. My mother humbly and respectfully promised Pharaoh's Daughter that she would properly nurse the child, and return him back to her as she instructed when he had been weaned. Then, with the greatest possible joy of heart and gladness ever, my mother and I departed the royal palace with my mother cradling the smallest member of our family pressed tightly yet tenderly and adoringly against her bosom. We both wept uncontrollably with sheer delight all the way home. Once again, our God had shown Himself to be the magnificent and caring God He had always promised to be and who had now so lovingly demonstrated His promise keeping greatness to us.

Time passed and that fateful day arrived. And on that day when Moses, as Pharaoh's Daughter had named him, was weaned, my mother took him back to the palace and into the arms and life of Pharaoh's Daughter to be raised as her own son from then on; to live in the palace of Pharaoh as a member of his household and family. I was not permitted to go with them on that journey, my mother wanted to spend those precious final moments alone with her youngest son.

But I often wondered what my mother talked to Moses about as they walked together back to the palace. How did she explain to him who he really was, that he was in fact a Hebrew, and that she was giving him away to another woman, an Egyptian woman, to be raised by this Egyptian as her son. It was a very sad and miserable day for me also as I thought I would never see my Moses again in life. After all, what reason would I have to visit the Royal Palace or be in the presence of those who lived in or near the palace? Further, what reason would my brother have to walk among or near the community of Israelites, the people from whom he came and to whom he really belonged? Would he even remember he was Hebrew? These thoughts plagued my mind, making me more miserable than I had ever been in life. I very quickly fell headlong into such a state of mourning which grew deeper as the days passed by, that I began to feel almost as if he had indeed actually died. And with each passing year I became more convinced that my fear of never seeing my younger brother again would be the very way I would live out my life. Furthermore each year at the time of his birth, I counted how old he had become and wondered what life had been like for our Moses whom God had spared and permitted to live in the very same palace with the evil-spirited Pharaoh who had decreed Moses should die at his birth.

As the years progressed, life in Egypt became almost unbearable. A new Pharaoh had come into power and the Hebrews were forced into very hard and tedious, backbreaking labor. In fact we had actually become slaves to the Egyptian government and the Egyptian people. Mixing clay and mud and combining it with straw and other straw-like particles for the sake of making bricks became the primary task required of the Hebrew men. The labor was intense, and the fact that it was done in the hot blazing sun with very few rest periods made the work that much more painful and torturous to the bodies of our Hebrew men. There was a great deal of tension, pain, mental and emotional anguish attached to living conditions of our people because of this work and way of life. We were constantly crying out to our God for our deliverance and it was our trust that He would one day hear our plea.

Then one day a rumor began to circulate about a young man from Pharaoh's house who had intervened on behalf of a Hebrew brick maker. It seems an Egyptian taskmaster was being particularly harsh to a Hebrew man beating him mercilessly, so that when the young man from Pharaoh's house witnessed the situation, he became enraged and defended the Hebrew with such force and strength against the Egyptian taskmaster that the taskmaster ended up dead on the ground. It took less than one day for the news of this matter to spread like a roaring fire out of control among the Hebrew people. My family and I spoke about this for hours on end during our evening meals; what could this mean? Why had someone from the house of Pharaoh defended one of our Hebrew men? Almost the whole of our community was talking about it and wondering what it all meant.

The rumor declared that the day following the taskmaster killing, two Hebrew men in the brick making fields became

85

engaged in a heated argument and the young man from Pharaoh's house saw this, approach them, reprimanded them, and asked why they were fighting between themselves considering they were brothers one to another as Hebrews. Hot-headed and inpatient, one of the argumentative Hebrew men flared up and shouted against the man from Pharaoh's house as to whether it was his plan to kill them also as he had killed the Egyptian the day before. Instantly, the young man from Pharaoh's house became fearful that because his previous day's deed had become known among the Hebrews it would surely also become known within the house of Pharaoh; and his life of Egyptian royalty and freedom would be in peril or perhaps even ended altogether. With this dread in mind the young man who had grown up in Pharaoh's house as a member of Pharaoh's family but who had protected a Hebrew man from the brutality of an Egyptian taskmaster, now suddenly realized he had to flee for his own life. He must leave the only home and comfort he remembered; the house of Pharaoh, ruler of Egypt.

As this story continued to circulate among us, it took on a life of its own and began to be looked upon as perhaps the answer to our prayers for deliverance from the enslaved conditions we were living in day after day. But as the years passed with no evidence of deliverance in sight, the mystery still lingered within our folklore of the day a man from Pharaoh's house defended one of our own. And for the next 40-years or so this story while remaining perplexing to us, became quite legendary within our collection of amazing episodes that formed the history of our Hebrew people.

Then strangely one evening without any previous warning, my brother Aaron told us the Lord had spoken to him and said that he was to go into the desert where he would meet our brother Moses. God said Moses had fled Egypt 40 years ago, and was now being sent back to Egypt. Aaron was to go out into the desert to meet him and return with him back to Egypt. Aaron being obedient to God began immediately gathering food and supplies in preparation to go into the desert to meet Moses as God had instructed him. I wanted to believe Aaron, but dared not allow my hopes to accept as truth that Aaron had heard God clearly. Uncertain that he had really heard from the Lord, but hoping that he had, we bade farewell to Aaron as he left us on his way into the desert to meet Moses and return back to Egypt with him.

When it seemed enough time had gone by we all began looking toward the desert in hopes of seeing the return of our brothers. While in the fields throughout the laborious workdays making bricks, the men of Israel looked toward the desert. During their daily chores of sundry arduous household duties, the women looked toward the desert. The elders who were not exempt from forceful and difficult tasks but who performed them with a dignity befitting an elder, gazed out toward the desert. At night during the darkness of the sky, watchmen were posted to look toward the desert.

And so it was with great delight that one day we could finally see far in the distance what appeared to be the shapes of the men returning home; shapes of men that we thought surely must be Aaron and Moses. Immediately we began making arrangements for the slaughtering of our most fatted young calves and baking breads in preparation for the festivities and merriment in anticipation of the joyous return of our long lost brother to us. And when at long last they had barely set their feet on the boundaries of our village, we ran out into the desert shouting and singing in masses, men, women, and children to meet them in welcoming gladness. This unexpected yet long hoped for return, marked the beginning of many nights of jubilant singing, dancing, worship and merriment after and in spite of each day's long hours of intense slave labor. Everything that was usually reserved for sacramental festivals including sacrifices and offerings was enjoyed for many nights after Moses' return. I was beside myself with unbelievable glee; our Moses, my baby brother was indeed alive and had come home after so many, many years away from us. During these festivities, we spent many hours listening to our Moses share with us what had become of him during his years away from his people. He confirmed that the tales of a man who once lived in Pharaoh's house but had run away from Pharaoh's house for his very life was not a fabled collection of rumors but instead was a story of truth. Moses told us he had fled to Midian and while there had found favor in the eyes of Reuel, the Priest of Midian who in turn had given his daughter Zipporah to Moses to be Moses' wife. After settling in Midian as a keeper of the flocks and being content to live there with his wife Zipporah and their son Gershom, Moses one day had a most unbelievable and amazing experience while tending his flocks. Finding himself on the backside of the desert at the mountain called Horeb, Moses witnessed a fire among the brush. The fire however was not alarming to Moses. Fires among the thickets were frequent occurrences amid some of the underbrush which were especially more prone than other shrub to become enflamed by the dry heat and burning sun of particularly hot days. But while observing the fire and expecting it to eventually burn itself out leaving the charred remains of bush particles, Moses was alarmed to notice that the fire continued to burn in full blaze, while the bush remained in its original state of lush green condition. In disbelief of what his eyes were beholding, Moses sought a closer look by moving nearer to the bush. Suddenly Moses said he heard his name being called, not from the air, but the calling of his name was coming directly from out of the bush itself. "Moses! Moses!" the voice called. Fearful yet curious,

Moses said he heard himself answer the bush, "Yes, I am here." Not knowing what was to come next with this conversation with a flaming bush that was not burning to cinders, but was rather remaining green and full, he waited in wonderment. He said he then heard the voice of our Lord demanding that he not come any closer to the bush but instead to remove his shoes because the ground upon which Moses was standing was holy. The voice continued Moses said, and identified itself as the God of Father Abraham, Father Isaac, and of Father Jacob. By this time Moses was filled with dread because he realized that by looking directly at and conversing with the flaming bush, he had been committing the forbidden act of looking at the face of God.

More fearful now than before, Moses hid his face in hopes his boldness would be forgiven and his life spared. The voice of God continued, saying he had seen the hardship of Abraham's descendants, had heard their cries, and knew their pain; and was now going to rescue them from the harsh hands of the Egyptians. Continuing, God told Moses He was going to take Abrahams descendants to another land that would be their own land, filled with honey and milk, and everything good that would bless them to flourish. God then said Moses would be the one to go into Egypt and bring his people out of Egypt so they could get to the land God was promising them. Moses listened in disbelief and terror because it had been his intention to never return to the land he fled so many years ago in fear for his life.

As we all sat and listened to Moses, we could barely believe what he was saying. Could it be that we were finally going to be set free from this burdensome slavery the Egyptians had inflicted upon us? We had indeed been praying for deliverance for so many years; but was it really going to happen as Moses was telling us it would? His news was too wonderful to believe, yet it filled us with such hope!

This God who had no name was now sharing His name with my brother and making promises to my brother concerning us. This once no-named God was now revealing Himself and His name to my brother as *"I AM."* Our Moses was to stand in the presence of the mighty Pharaoh of Egypt and declare to him that he should release the enslaved Israelites from bondage forever, because *"I AM"* said so. Such loud and hopeful rejoicing erupted throughout our camps as we listened to Moses' promises. And because of Moses' promises, the music and dancing, and worship continued until almost dawn. And even though we began each day of enslaved hardship with tired bodies from much celebrating the night before, our hearts and spirits were light and encouraged because we believed Moses' promises would come to pass.

But among all of us within the camps, I believe I was the most glad about the return of Moses; my baby brother had been returned to me. My years of wondering, crying, aching, and sadness had now come to an end because I could finally behold my brother with my own eyes and touch him once again.

There were many set-backs as we attempted to leave Egypt. Pharaoh would make a declaration that we could leave in peace, but would change his mind at the precise time we were to leave and we would be forced to remain. For so very long we endured so many of Pharaoh's mind changes one right after another. And with each of his decisions of refusal to let us be free, our God would send a most awful plague against Pharaoh and all of Egypt. Finally after ten terrible acts of God against Pharaoh, we were released from our oppressive captivity, to go out from Egyptian bondage and into the unknown destination of safety and freedom under the leading and direction of my brother Moses.

But our joy at being set free was short lived when it became clear that Pharaoh's hard heartedness had once again raised its awful head resulting in yet another change of mind. He wanted us back in Egypt under his tyrannical rule, and had therefore mustered his mighty army in full pursuit after us to force us back into slavery. But my brother Moses was fearless in the face of this unexpected set-back. To him, this was not a set-back at all, but an opportunity to witness and experience the tremendous hand of God to intervene on our behalf. I am still amazed as I recall how God so magnificently rescued us from Pharaoh's hand. Our God literally opened the mouth of the Red Sea and bade us come and walk through. Imagine my sisters-in-time if you can, I actually walked on the firm and dry bed of the Red Sea. Forever burned into my memory, I can almost experience it all over again as if it just happened this morning, walking on the dry ground of the sea that presented itself as a long, splendid and glorious Palace corridor taking us to another place of security and protection. And the walls of this very fine palace corridor were the rippling, cool waters of the Red Sea, standing tall at attention bidding us to come and walk through, as they positioned themselves alongside us to be our grand and majestic wall of protection. What a beautiful and heart throbbing occurrence, I shall never forget it. But again in the midst of our joy, came the frightening sight of Pharaoh's army racing after us. But our God, Oh our wonderful, protective God, demonstrated His unmatched power again right before our eyes. Once we had made it safely onto the opposite shores of the Red Sea, those once protective Red Sea walls which had held themselves upright for us, suddenly collapsed with a rushing force right onto Pharaoh's army drowning them in a spinning whirl of overpowering water. Realizing we had yet again been kept safe from capture, there arose a deafening, roaring shout of praise and worship to our God for delivering us one more

91

time. Would He continue to deliver us out of impossible and death threatening circumstances like these over and over? I can't hold back my tears now even as I share this experience with you my sisters, of God's loving and defending hand upon us time after time.

Our journey to the place where Moses was taking us became taxing and arduous for him because our people complained constantly about almost everything. Despite the fact that our God fed us with food that He sent from heaven, and which we did not need to plant or harvest; and despite another fact that our feet never became swollen or blistered; or that our sandals and clothes never wore out, we still found reasons to grumble and complain. Some even dared suggest that Moses was not the only one who could lead us that somehow God could speak to any one of us as well. I am now so ashamed to confess to you my sisters that I became one of those who complained and spoke out against my own brother, my beloved Moses. How he bore our criticisms, protests and whining, I will never know.

Even my eldest brother Aaron and I complained about Moses. We were not at all happy about our Moses marrying a Cushite woman. We wanted him to choose a wife from among the beautiful Hebrew woman all of whom would no doubt have been more than eager to become his bride. So Aaron and I expressed our disapproval about the matter. But God made His displeasure very clear of our accusations against His cherished Moses. He called the three of us out of the tent, Moses, Aaron and I. Then He made Aaron and I step forward and severely reprimanded us about our attitude and behavior against Moses. He made it clear that He speaks to Moses and not to us. And further, that the way He speaks to Moses is not His usual way of speaking to prophets through visions, dreams and riddles, but that when He speaks to

Moses, He does so face-to-face. When God finished His rebuke, and His cloud lifted, I was horrified to see that my skin had become white with leprosy. When Aaron also saw it, he pleaded with Moses to speak to God on my behalf. And as usual, my loving and caring Moses asked God for mercy for my healing. God replied that I should first be isolated away from everyone to a secluded place outside of the camp for 7 days after which I would be healed and could be brought back among the people into the camp. I learned my lesson well from that experience and wrote a letter to my Moses as an act of repentance and explanation for my behavior. This is what I said in the letter.

My Dearest Brother Moses:

I begin this letter with an apology. In allowing myself to be persuaded by my emotions, my jealousy and personal biases against Ethiopian people, I said some very unkind things about you, your relationship with our God and your choice for a wife. But because you are a man of kindness and humility, I believe you will forgive my impudent tongue and ungrateful heart. I regret hurting you and can offer no sufficient excuses. But, permit me my dear brother to explain how deeply I love you and why I did what I did and said what I said.

The day you were born our home was filled with delight mixed with sadness because of Pharaoh's ruling that all newborn Hebrew males were to be killed. We wept bitterly but still we sought God for an escape from Pharaoh's edict. Mother conceived the idea of the floating basket, Father hand-crafted it and I was designated to watch over you while you floated on the Nile River in the warmth and safety of your basket. Every day as I waded in the water beside you in your little basket, I sang Hebrew lullabies to you and told you stories of Fathers Abraham, Isaac and Jacob and how we came to be in Egypt. On the day we wandered near Pharaoh's Daughter, she discovered you tucked inside the basket and immediately loved you and instantly decided to keep you as her own son. Heartbroken at the thought of never seeing you again, I spoke up to Pharaoh's Daughter and offered to take you to a Hebrew woman who could nurse and wean you. I also told her with broken heart that the woman would even return you to her at a later time after the completion of your weaning. Because she agreed to my offer I was elated that I would have you still in my life even if just a short while longer. I reasoned that a short while was better than no time at all.

So, when you were weaned and returned to Pharaoh's Daughter, our family wept again and again but we prayed to God to preserve you. Imagine my delight when after so many years you returned, all grown up, handsome, masterful and holding the most inconceivable position ever. You had come to lead our people from the same bondage which had sought to snuff out your infant life. I am proud of you my dear brother and I admit to being a little overprotective of you and certainly somewhat discontented at having to share you with so many others. I know that our God has His hand on your life even now just as He did when you were first born. So Moses my dear brother please know that my words against you were the foolish rantings of a jealous older sister who silently and secretly wished to return to a time when she had you all to herself in the warm and gentle waters of the Nile River singing lullabies to you. Forgive me Moses.
Forever your loving Sister,
Miriam

As we continued on our journey across the hot sands of the desert for many more years, and through many more towns and cities, I never raised a complaining voice against Moses ever again. When we reached a location known as the desert of Zin at a place called Kadesh, I was feeling particularly weary after so many wandering years. So, my dear Jennifer, it was there at Kadesh that I drew my last breath and died. I was buried there. Since that time I had rested in the world of the dead for millennia until the day I met Him again. It was Jesus. I remembered Him from the time before time when I existed in the mind of God, and Jesus was present with God, He was present as God. So, I knew Him immediately when I saw Him again, I knew His voice when I heard it again. The many, many years had not altered the kindness and peace in His voice. How could my ears not recall with serene and welcoming memory, the sound of His wonderful voice? He was holding a set of keys in His hand and said He was releasing all in the realm of the dead who wished to be released. He was permitting them to go into a place of paradise where they will wait in comfort for Jesus's next earthly visit. He said He would surely return again at a later time and would then take all of us back with Him to our new home, a home of eternal substance and existence. So when I and my sisters leave you Jennifer, we are all going back to our wonderful place of waiting as we abide there with confidence that He who promised to come again for us, will surely come, just as He said He would.

Chapter 7
I Was Not Drunk

Hannah's voice was soft as were the others but there was something in her tone a little different than all the rest. She sounded as if she felt the need to convince everyone that she indeed was a woman of sobriety. "I was not drunk as Priest Eli supposed I was," she said defensively. The two women seated on either side of her put their arms around her and whispered comfortingly into her ears. Hannah's eyes brimmed with tears as she tried to continue, and another woman from across the room came over to her and with the corner of her shawl wiped away Hannah's tears. Then another of the women said gently, "It's alright my dear, we know the truth and so do you, so never mind his accusations." Hannah seemed to gain strength from her sisters-in-time and repositioned herself a little straighter to proceed with her story. "He thought I was drunk, but I was not," she repeated, but with more confidence this time. I was so intent in my prayers that I was reeling on my knees and my tears were uncontrollable, that's when I heard him ask me how long I was going to stay drunk and even commanded that I put away my wine and stop drinking. Hannah paused and took in a long deep breath and placed both her hands on her lips to conceal their quivering. "There, there,..." said one of the other women as she gently patted Hannah's knee, "you have come a long distance dear to tell your story." It appeared Hannah was the sensitive one among them but she felt safety and comfort in the company of the other women. So once again, she straightened herself, lifted her drooping shoulders and tried yet once more to go on with her story.

Hannah had been married to Elkanah who was a good man and a very caring and generous husband. He had spared no opportunity to lavish gifts upon Hannah and to make displays of kind benevolence toward her. But the generosity from Elkanah was frequently offset by the hurtful actions and comments of his other wife Peninnah who took delight in Hannah's inability to bear children. Hannah was barren. While Peninnah was fertile and had given Elkanah several sons, Hannah had given him no children at all, not so much as even a girl child. Her inability to conceive had left Hannah with a feeling of overwhelming emptiness and a sense of depressing uselessness. Almost every contact or conversation with Peninnah left Hannah in bitter tears. She tried to shield herself from Peninnah's chides and avoid her reproaches but to no avail because Peninnah was never too far away and was always ready to spew out a biting comment. In Hannah's efforts to console herself with the knowledge of her husband's abiding love for her, she imagined that she would one day repay his love by conceiving and giving her beloved husband a son. But at times out of sheer despairing fretfulness, Hannah would go so far as to deny herself food or drink for days at a time. And in her most desperate moments, she would collapse into the arms of her husband in a weeping frenzy. Elkanah was at his wits end during these occurrences and asked Hannah if he alone was not sufficient enough to bring her happiness? After all hadn't he been generous and given her all that he could, did he not mean more to her than ten sons? This was the kind of emotional upheaval and turmoil that filled Hannah's days year after year.

Finally, on one of her husband's yearly trips to Shiloh to worship and sacrifice to the Lord, Hannah accompanied him and entered into the Temple herself to beseech the Lord for a child. She was willing to beg God for a child and had already determined in her mind to do just that. She even decided to go so far as to offer God a bargain, that if He would open her womb and permit her to conceive, she was prepared to promise God that she would give Him back the child, if He would only...

It was during this trip that Hannah came face to face with Eli the Priest. She didn't offer the Priest an explanation for her presence in the Temple rather she simply entered the Temple and immediately began her plaintive and desperate appeal to her all-knowing and perfect God. As she knelt and cried and swayed, Eli caught sight of her and concluded she had taken far too much wine before coming to Temple. Here is where he accused Hannah of being drunk and here also is where Hannah felt Eli's blatant charge, it was the final sharp dagger of pain into her heart. She was devastated that the Priest neither tried to understand her suffering, nor considered a more humane or less derogatory cause for her weeping. Instead, he had accused her of a most demeaning offense, excessive consumption of wine. At this she could only utter her response to his indictment in barely audible tones, "I am not drunk...I am pouring out my soul to my God...I am deeply anguished...and I am not drunk." Eli the Priest offered no apology for misinterpreting Hannah's state of mind nor did he acknowledge his incorrect allegation, he simply told her to go in peace and offered hopes that God would grant her what she had asked.

Hannah completed her prayers as best she could under the circumstances and left the Temple. Once outside in the open air, she noticed that she felt quite a bit better, she felt lighter and realized her appetite had returned. She took a seat near the far end of the Temple courtyard and waited for her husband to complete his worship and sacrifice rituals. As she sat she felt quite a bit more relaxed than before. She lifted her face to the sun, closed her eyes and soaked in the warmth of the sun's rays which seemed to bathe and comfort her with a sense of peacefulness and calm.

Early the next morning, after worshipping before the Lord, Hannah and Elkanah packed up their belongings to prepare for their two-day journey back home to Ramah. Hannah was still feeling lighthearted and peaceful and noticed an absence of the usual fretfulness she felt whenever in Peninnah's company. In fact she was able to return a warm smile to Peninnah's mocking glares. But at about midmorning just before the time of departure back to Ramah, Elkanah, in an unusual move, came into Hannah's tent with a particularly beguiling look on his face. Hannah knew the look, she was familiar with it, but she had not ever seen it before during their yearly trips to the Temple at Shiloh. Elkanah was usually very distant and in deep thought after Temple as if he was still in the presence of the Lord. But now, the sly looking smile on his face with his lips barely parted, was very much like the look he often gave her when entering her tent after an intensely long day in the field. How very well she recognized the look, and how very excited she was to see it now. As Hannah recalled the incident, she began to blush and turned her head aside in an effort to hide her face. But it was of no use, the women in the room all knew what Hannah was about to share, and they waited with eager anticipation to hear the details. Hannah managed to tell her story of that exciting coming together with Elkanah; of all the times they had done so, that noteworthy instance had become for Hannah the one most memorable and scintillating throughout her and Elkanah's life together. It was from that union that Hannah conceived her first child, the child she had so longed for and begged God for.

The glares and biting comments from Peninnah ceased the moment it was known that Hannah was bearing a child. And Hannah was delighted beyond what she had ever imagined she could be as she carried and finally gave birth to her first son, whom she named Samuel because she said, "I asked the LORD for him." And so it was, that the following year when Elkanah went up to offer the annual sacrifice to the LORD and to fulfill his vow in the Temple, Hannah did not go. She told Elkanah she was not going to accompany him this time because the child was not yet weaned, but she would accompany him after some time when the young boy had been fully weaned.

Hannah shared, that when the time came about for her young Samuel to be completely weaned, she was anticipating with great delight her annual trip with Elkanah to the Temple, for two very exciting reasons. The first reason was that she would be able to keep her vow to her gracious and caring God for delivering her a son. She had promised God during that painful prayer in the Temple a few years prior that if God would so favor her with a child she would in all gratefulness give the child back to the God who had heard and granted her plea. She would completely surrender her beloved and longed for child to the Lord to live forever in the service of the Lord under the guidance of Eli, the priest of God who had falsely accused her of being overcome with much wine. Hannah's second cause for delight in returning to the Temple was for the pleasure she would receive when she delivered her precious son to Priest Eli and remind him that she was in fact certainly not under the influence of new wine as he had so blatantly accused her. However, although Hannah enjoyed tremendously the moment she confronted Eli with the tangible outcome of her prayer, she was not disrespectful to him. She very carefully chose her words, "Pardon me man of God, I am the woman who knelt here praying to the LORD for this child, and as you can see, the LORD has granted me what I asked of Him. And now, just as I promised during that prayer when you mistakenly thought I was drunk, I am now giving him back to the LORD so that for his entire life he is to be dedicated to the LORD to serve Him always; and I am leaving him here with you to be taught by you how to serve our God." At this juncture in her explanation of the interaction she had with Prophet Eli, Hannah paused briefly in respect for the seriousness of the subject, and to demonstrate appreciation to God for His blessing in Samuel. After a few respectful moments, Hannah giggled outright. She could not hold back how enjoyable and amusing it had been to remind Prophet Eli face-to-face of how in error he had been when he so unceremoniously reproached her with his indictment of excessive wine intake. It served him right she said. Then as spontaneous laughter filled the room from the other women in defense and agreement with Hannah's actions toward Eli, Hannah herself gained strength and was now completely at ease continuing her story; "drunk indeed," she exclaimed with a new vigor. For much too long Hannah had needed to be free from that age old allegation, and it seemed that now after so many millennia, she was finally free.

As Hannah continued her story, she never ceased to give God glory for hearing her prayer and obliging her prayerful request by granting her exactly what she had asked for, a child. In fact, the loving response of her prayer answering God became the center of Hannah's existence and her joy after giving birth to Samuel. God heard her, and He answered her, and that fact pleased Hannah to a greater degree than she was able to express in words. And so it was with an even more grateful heart that Hannah received the life-giving blessings from her God in the form of six more children. How wonderful God had been to her, a once barren woman unable to conceive and bear any children at all, to a woman who would give birth to seven children. God was gracious to Hannah and she in her desire to show God how much she appreciated His generosity, wrote a prayer expressing her thankfulness. Also, it was her hope that her prayer would become a source of encouragement to other barren women. She closed her eyes, raised her hands and began quoting the first few words of her prayer. *My heart rejoices in the LORD; my mouth boasts over my enemies, for I delight in my deliverance O God.* At this point in her prayer, Hannah began to insert a plaintive yet joyful melody to her prayer; then with the precision of a finely tuned, well-rehearsed chorus, the other women joined in and sang together in beautiful harmony Hannah's song. *There is no one holy like the LORD; there is no one besides Him; there is no Rock like our God.* Jennifer's eyes widened. Had they rehearsed Hannah's song prior to their visit? But just as soon as the thought entered her mind, Jennifer found herself also joining in the singing as if she too knew the lyrics and melody despite having never heard them before. And although this whole matter puzzled her, Jennifer nonetheless continued in song, *For You Lord are the God who knows, and by You all deeds are weighed. She who was barren has borne seven children, You guarded the feet of Your servant. It is not by my strength that I prevailed, but by Your strength alone O LORD, Most High. You gave me strength and You heard my prayer.* The singing fortified Jennifer; she felt a calming reassurance from the lyrics and experienced a strong bonding and fellowship with these brave and wonderful women who had entered her world from the past to visit her and share their stories. This must be what real sisterhood is all about and what it most likely will feel like when we all reach heaven and join together in song about our one God who loves us all so very much.

As if reading Jennifer's mind, Hannah looked directly into Jennifer's eyes and said, "Yes my dear, you are right."

Chapter 8
My Son Was Hebrew

Good evening Jennifer dear, I am Hagar, an Egyptian. I was Sarai's slave, her maidservant. I was part of the very large clan of people who were the personal household servants and field-hands owned by my lord Abram. Although we were a very large group, we were a closely knit clan of people who genuinely loved and cared for one another. This closeness was especially evident during the evenings when the major chores had been completed, the evening meal had been consumed and we relaxed around several fires spread throughout our camp. We enjoyed the company of one another and the conversations about the day's events, and how our animals were faring and multiplying and breeding. There were always throngs of children milling about, playing, running in and out of the tents, and chasing sparks from the fires. The older children shared their stories as well or otherwise participated with the adults in singing the campfire songs.

By introducing myself as an enslaved person Jennifer, I am doing so just to make it clear that during those times, enslaving groups of people was a common practice among the many tribes and clans who lived then. The stronger people would overtake and capture the weaker ones and press them into bondage and servitude. After a war, and there were many, the victorious ones would almost always force the defeated people into a state of slavery. And so that was my place in life as an adult because I and a large group of my people were spared when the Israelites conducted a mass slaughtering of Egyptians. Those of us who were spared were then taken by force into the Israelite nation as their slaves after the war between my people and my lord Abram, who was the most powerful Israelite of that time. While my sisters, cousins and other relatives were dispersed throughout the huge population of Israelites, I was given to Sarai to be her personal slave and handmaiden for her every bidding.

At this point in her narrative, Hagar glanced over at Sarai who was sitting with her head bowed and her eyes closed. The atmosphere in the room became somewhat strained; the tension between Hagar and Sarai was evident. There was silence in the room for a long period while no one uttered a word. It seemed necessary for Hagar and Sarai to be the ones to initiate reconciliation of the conflict between them. They were the only ones who could. Everyone in the room sat motionless allowing time to be the initiator of whatever was to come of the awkward relationship between these two women. Jennifer felt tempted to be the first to break the silence, but a stern glance from Lot's wife put a halt to any thought of Jennifer's intent to intervene. Sarai did not look up from her bowed head position while Hagar continued to look to Sarai for some sign of emotional response. Seeing no reaction forthcoming from Sarai, Hagar regained her composure and proceeded with her story.

She slipped into a verbal stroll down memory lane of her childhood days in Egypt. I had grown up in a fairly well-off household which enjoyed almost all the comforts that Egyptian living could afford. In fact, I myself had handmaidens to provide my every personal need, and my family maintained several other male and female house servants. I had been educated by some of Egypt's most well respected scholars. And it was because my father was a believer in equal education for both his daughters and his sons that I and my sisters received our academic instruction together with our brothers in the same learning temple.
Hagar's face literally beamed as she recalled the days of her youth before her capture by the Israelites. But it was the outcome of the battle between my people and the Israelite people that determined my fate. The Egyptian army lost the war against Israel's fighting men, and it was because of this loss that I would be separated from my family. I was left with

only memories of a previous life as a free woman living in comfort in Egypt because I had been reduced to the lowly status of an enslaved handmaiden to an Israelite woman. But such was life and that's what my life had become.

It was a well-known fact that Israelite women were prolific child bearers, Hagar reported. There were many, many children within the Israelite camp, therefore it was puzzling to me that Sarai had not yet provided her husband Abram with a child. So when rumors began to spread throughout the camp that Sarai had been promised by the Israelite's God that she would give birth soon, I was completely mystified by this unbelievable promise. Although this God of Israel had already proven Himself to be far superior to all the other gods of the surrounding nations, the idea of a woman giving birth at Sarai's age seemed too impossible even for Israel's God. Sarai was very close to 80 years old and Abram was close to 90, so how could this rumor be anything other than just that, a rumor, or perhaps the result of someone's wild and unrealistic imagination. But it was the talk of the camp. There was a day that I shall never forget. It was the day Sarai came to me and told me that because of the promise of her God, she had determined His promise was to come through me, her handmaiden. And since I belonged to Sarai, anything I did was the same as if she had done it; anything I owned was also hers. That ownership had no boundaries, it even included any children I should bear, because the children I gave birth to would be the same as if she had given them birth. So in Sarai's haste to bring her God's promise into being, she sent her husband, lord Abram into my tent so that I would conceive through him and thus make it possible for her God's promise to come to pass.

At this point in her story, Hagar turned and caught a glimpse of Sarai's visible anguish; Sarai was clearly having a difficult time listening to Hagar's account of what happened between her and Abram. The two women's eyes met and Hagar took the opportunity to express something she had been holding in for so long. Forgive me Sarai for saying this, but you sent your husband in to sleep with me at a time when he was old and declining in his ability to bring pleasure to a woman. Yet you sent him to me. And having never cast my eyes on his appendage of manhood before this time, my guess was that what I saw at the time he came in to me was probably a fading image of a formerly robust and fully bloomed specimen of a strong limb any man would have been proud to display, and any woman would have been eager to experience. But I was not so eager, yet I had no choice. Here again, Sarai dropped her head and looked away from Hagar.

Hagar went on with her story. The first time lord Abram came into my tent, he sat on the side of my bed and explained that this arrangement was not his idea, that he was simply going along with his wife Sarai's plan to bring forth the children God had promised would be brought forth. It sounded almost as if he was apologizing for coming into my tent without my invitation, but I quickly dismissed that notion because the men of our day in all the cultures, never apologized to women. Not for any reason. This was my first time being this close to lord Abram. He was usually in the field, or with the men of the camp, fighting a battle with a neighboring culture, or otherwise too busy to notice or talk to me. But I soon realized he was not like the other men in our camp or like other men I had been around or known. He was not arrogant or brutal and he did not force himself onto me as I expected. I had seen how strong, and forceful he could be in situations of combat, but I saw none of those

112

characteristics when he came into my tent. He would always engage me in conversation first and permit me to relax before arranging myself in readiness for him. And so it was that every time we came together I was completely taken by delightful surprise because of his gentleness and even more surprised by his manliness which was never lacking in strength or purpose. I soon found myself wondering what he might have been like in his youthful days considering his present state of pleasurable ability and skill. He was never at a loss, and I actually enjoyed with much satisfaction, his visits. However, as soon as it was clear that I had conceived, his visits came to an abrupt halt.

Hagar admitted to being very angry, disappointed and saddened when Abram's visits ceased. She said she had enjoyed and anticipated Abram's visits and decided to use the only thing at her disposal to express her feelings, her pregnancy. So, as each month progressed and the swelling evidence of her pregnancy also progressed, Hagar flaunted herself around and throughout the camp and especially in the presence of Sarai. Hagar said it became very clear that both she and Sarai were experiencing regrets and resentments. Sarai regretted sending Abram into Hagar's tent, and Hagar resented Sarai for being the wife of the man Hagar had come to genuinely like, perhaps even to love. Her only comfort now was that she carried Abram's seed and Sarai did not. But it didn't take very long Hagar said, before she realized that her flaunting bore her a serious price. Sarai took every opportunity to remind Hagar that her pregnancy did not change the fact that Hagar was still just a handmaiden, and Sarai was the one with the authority. Sarai's severe and harsh tasking of Hagar made Hagar realize that her boastful displays had cost her a great deal more than she thought it would.

The tension in the room mounted as Hagar continued her story. Jennifer struggled to adjust to the friction in the air, but quickly realized she would simply have to endure the uneasiness she was feeling. And looking around her room she could see that everyone else was uneasy as well, but no one attempted to curb or subdue Hagar's retelling of her experiences; after-all, wasn't this the reason they had all come; to tell their stories?

Hagar went on. I felt I could no longer live under those intense conditions so I did the only thing I knew how to do, I ran away. I ran away into the desert to live alone until my child was born and then I would make a home for us there in the desert. But Abram's God met me as I sat weeping near a spring of water in the desert. This God asked me where I was going and why I was weeping. I told Him I was weeping out of my deep sadness; that I was sad because I was no longer a part of the huge family of Abram which had been my home and my family for so very long. And I was also sad because I was now alone with my unborn child not knowing what to do or where in the desert I should go. Then Abram's God told me to return to Sarai. Somehow, I was not surprised that Abram and Sarai's God would tell me to return to the very people from whom I had just fled. I reasoned that since He was Sarai's God and not mine, He favored them over me because He was their God. Then as if He heard my thoughts, He said to me, *"I have no favorites among humanity Hagar. I love them all because I made them all. But I am telling you to return because it is not safe out here in the desert for you, a woman, alone, with child, and soon with no more provisions. You have neither a tent of your own nor men around you to protect you from other nations and predators who would most certainly do more harm to you than Sarai ever could. Go back to Sarai where you will be safe, and stop flaunting yourself in front of her. You will bear a son whom you will name Ishmael. He will be a wild and unruly man, not getting along with anyone in or outside of his family; but from him you will become the mother of many, many people, too many for you to count. Now go back to Abram's camp, there is safety there."*

At this point in her narrative, Hagar, began to cry and sway. She said, I gave this God of Abram a name. I said to Him, You are the God who sees me in my distress and who also understands me. And now I have seen the One who sees me. And He answered me saying, *"Yes, I see you now, I have always seen you and I have always loved you, now go back to your place of safety."* I felt as if He was now my God also, so loving and so caring. He was no longer just the God of Abram's people, but He was now also mine to love and worship.

So, I went back to Sarai and the safety of Abram's camp. I stopped flaunting myself as my new God told me, and before long my man-child was born just as God said. I told Abram of my experience in the desert and of the name God told me to give to our son. Abram was pleased. He accepted the name Ishmael and was delighted at his new status as a father, he was proud that this son had come directly from his own loins. Despite the fact that culturally every man-child born within his camp belonged to him and was considered his son, Abram could now say with much pride that this son was in reality his very own. He could make this claim not based on his status as lord of the nation he was leading, or by the fact that everything and everyone within the camp belonged to him, but because it was from his own issue that this man-child had been conceived and born. Thus, Abram made no attempts to conceal his delight in the son to whom God Himself had given the name Ishmael.

Ishmael grew up within the community as a privileged boy because he was the son of Abram. When Ishmael was 13-years old, his father Abram who was 99 years-old came to us with two very strange and unusual plans which he said God had instructed him to put into place. The first thing was to have all the males from the age of13-years old and up to become what he called circumcised. All other males under 13 would not be circumcised until they reached the age of 13 and every male child born among us from this time on would be circumcised at 8-days old. This circumcision was a very bloody and severely painful process for the men. It required the skin which covered the tip of the male organ to be cut completely off without cutting off the tip of the organ itself. How was that to be done I wondered? I could only imagine what careful and exact cutting would need to be done. The men and young boys suffered tremendously from this procedure which Abram and just a few of his selected men performed. Then when all but the selected cutters had been circumcised, they were given the responsibility of performing the same cutting on each other as they had done for the rest of the male population. Abram did not excuse himself from this procedure, he ordered his own cutting to be done by one of the selected men. This entire process took many months to complete, as the cutting had to be done in stages and groups due to the many males within the family of Abram. Also, each group of men needed sufficient time to heal and recover from this painful ordeal before each next group could be circumcised. Abram told us God had ordered this blood stained action not only for our family of men alone, but it was to continue for every male within every generation yet to come. I was in deep agony and ached terribly for my 13-year old son Ishmael who was included in this bloody torment initiated by his father Abram. But with much heartbreak and suffering, we survived this time of stress and pain and I comforted my son in the best way I

116

knew how. I kept his bed covered with the softest skins available so he could rest with the least discomfort; I attended to his needs and prepared his food, even fed him myself if I thought he was too weak and in too much pain to feed himself.

The second strange thing Abram did, which he said had also been ordered by God, was to change his and Sarai's names. Neither he nor Sarai were to be known any longer by the names given to them by their fathers. He was to be known by the name of Abraham instead of Abram and Sarai was no longer to be known as Sarai but Sarah. It is for this reason that everyone now calls them Abraham and Sarah instead of their former names Abram and Sarai.

Eventually, everything seemed to settle back into our routine way of living. The bloody circumcision ritual was over, the men had survived and we were all mending from what seemed to have been a terrible blood drenched nightmare. When out of nowhere, the old rumor of Sarah bringing forth a child of her own, surfaced once again. We all thought God's promise to Abraham that he and Sarah would have a son had been fulfilled through me. It was for that reason that no further thought or discussion was given to the promise. But here it was 14-years later, and the promise resurfaced. This time it came up because Abraham told us that God had sent three men to visit him who had again repeated the promise, but this time with the understanding that Ishmael was not the promised son. The promised son would indeed come through Sarah herself and not her handmaid. This was to happen in 1 year. No one in the family could believe what we were hearing especially since Sarah was 89-years old. So, the only thing to do was to wait and see.

If we thought we could not believe our ears about Sarah giving birth in her old age, we clearly could not believe our eyes when she began to appear very definitely with child. But, as God had promised Abraham, Sarah soon gave birth to a male child whom Abraham named Isaac as God had instructed.

Pausing for a moment in her story, Hagar looked over at Sarah, and then around the room at the rest of the women to see how they were all responding to her account of her experiences as a slave woman within the camp of Abraham's people. Hagar then glanced again at Sarah and asked if she was feeling alright with her retelling of the circumstances as she had lived them. Sarah nodded without smiling and gestured for Hagar to continue. After all, this was the reason for their visit with Jennifer, to tell their stories as they had evolved in each of their lives. So Hagar reached over to Sarah and told her there was no need for either of them to be concerned now because it was clear that everything which had happened so long ago was meant to be. Sarah looked back at Hagar with a consenting expression and managed a weak but genuine smile.

Hagar continued. It was not long before little Isaac was weaned; and one day while playing with his brother Ishmael, Sarah became visibly displeased and determined it was now time for me and Ishmael to be sent away. Abraham did not intervene for me or his son but agreed with Sarah that I and Ishmael should go away. He packed us some provisions, a little food and some water and sent us away into the desert. I cannot know where he or Sarah thought we would go or how we would survive alone in the desert with such a small amount of provisions, and food and water. Surely they must have known that those items would soon run out; what would we do when that happened?   But I remembered my experience when I ran away 14-years earlier while I was still with child and I met Abraham's God who came to me with comforting words. Could it be that He would appear to me again? It was my hope that He would. After being cast out of the only family that Ishmael had ever known and the one which had been mine for more than half my life, he and I wandered in the desert until all our provisions were gone and we had nothing left to eat and no water to drink. I found myself desperate and in such deep despair, knowing that I and my son were about to die there in the desert. We had become very weak and barely able to put one foot in front of the other. I knew death was waiting nearby, so in my effort to make Ishmael's death as quick and painless as I could, I placed him under the shade of a small bush, kissed him, rubbed his frail body and turned quickly away to hide my tears from him. Without looking back I walked a short distance away so as not to witness the drawing of his last breath. There I sat in a crumbled heap weeping uncontrollably for my son whose life was being cut so short for no fault of his own.

At this point in her story telling, Hagar's voice quivered and halted, and the tears were streaming freely down her face. The other women in the room were also quite shaken by her narration. While indeed they each had endured horrible experiences, the knowledge of a suffering child aroused their maternal instincts and they responded as any loving mother would at the notion of a hurting child. Sarah also was shaken by this. She had not been witness to what occurred in the desert with Hagar and Ishmael, so that now as she listened to the terrifying account of the suffering they endured in the desert, Sarah was dismayed and severely saddened, and feeling quite a deep sense of guilt. Hagar, seeing Sarah's remorseful countenance gave her a reassuring nod that all was well and guilt was no longer necessary.

Continuing with her story, Hagar's own countenance began to change from that of a tense and anxious demeanor to a more tranquil, even pleasant expression. As sure as I had hoped, Hagar said, God met me again there in the desert just as He had 14-years earlier. He told me He had heard my son Ishmael's cries and mine as well and asked me why I was crying. His question to me sounded as if I should not have been upset, as though I should have known He would not leave me stranded in the desert. Surely if He rescued me those many years ago before my son was born, He would certainly rescue me again now that my son was in his youthful manhood. After all God had told me long ago what kind of man my Ishmael would become, a wild man dwelling in the presence of his brethren. Maybe it was the beginnings of his wildness that we saw in his playful behaviors with his brother Isaac. As Hagar recounted her experience in the desert with God, she literally sat up quite a bit straighter. Her confident upright posture matched her facial expression of assurance as she shared how God instructed her to lift Ishmael from his position on the ground, open her own eyes and see the deep well of cool refreshing water and give some to Ishmael so he could be revived and strengthened. Hagar said she filled her empty water jar with the cool well water, gave some to her son and watched him revive in just a matter of moments. She said she then took Ishmael by the hand and walked with him fully reassured, further into the desert to make a life for herself and her son. Now with her face aglow with smiles of delightful bliss, Hagar shared how she and Ishmael became desert dwellers, that Ishmael had become an excellent archer, in fact the best in the entire region which included the vast territory of Egypt, Hagar's place of birth. Thus, it was from Egypt that Hagar selected a wife for Ishmael. Hagar, Ishmael, and his wife prospered and did quite well in the desert wilderness. Ishmael's family grew to huge proportions just as God had promised and Hagar lived contentedly to a good old age surrounded by her son, her daughter-in-law, her grandchildren and several generations of Ishmael's offspring. Ishmael was becoming the father of a great nation, just as God told her he would.

Turning her attention to Jennifer, Hagar said, "you see Jennifer, I was more than just a servant girl who was used as a substitute for a promise from God. Instead of being simply a replacement, I became the mother of a great nation of people who grew and covered many parts of the earth and who still exist to this day, even here in your country which is very far away from where our lives unfolded." Hagar gestured to all the women in the room and said, we know of your struggles Jennifer dear, that's why we have come tonight. We are here to encourage you with our own stories, the stories which have not been included in any of the sacred texts of your time. You must remember what we tell you tonight, you must not ever forget.

Chapter 9
A Ludicrous Promise

Sarai began. Our God, our Most Magnificent, Beneficent, Faithful and Sovereign God, was always making the most unbelievable promises to us. However wonderful and exciting these promises were, they were also the most difficult to believe or even make sense of. His promises always went against everything we knew to be true and they stood out against everything that had ever been a part of anything we had experienced. Yet even despite all of this, His promises never failed to come to pass. And try as we may, we could not fathom how these wonderful things came to be nor could we explain them nor make any reasonable sense out of their appearance right at the exact time our wonderful God told us they would appear. But this promise I am about to share is personally the most outrageous of them all. I am Sarah, previously known as Sarai before God changed my name. The promise God made me was ludicrous indeed. But before I begin my story, I must first ask you for your forgiveness Hagar. I know that I thrust my husband, my lord Abram upon you, but I did so out of sheer desperation. At the time I thought I was making the right decision to bear children through you. I reasoned that would be the manner by which our God would exercise His promise. Then, after you gave birth to your beautiful son, I was jealous. That's why I sent you away into the desert. I could not bear to witness your happiness and the delight my lord husband Abram took in being with Ishmael, the son brought forth because the two of you had come together. But I was wrong, so please find it in your heart to forgive me. With grateful tears in her eyes Hagar spoke gently as she responded to Sarai, "Of course, my dear sister, I forgive you…but I do so only on the condition that you also forgive me for my unkind attitude toward you. I too was jealous, after all, my lord and master Abram was really your husband not mine. And I knew without a doubt that he loved only you." At once Hagar and Sarai spontaneously fell into an emotional embrace and sobbed softly into each other's arms. One of the women spoke up and said, "finally!" "Shhhh…" spoke several other women in unison. Another admonished, "Let them have their moment, this has been a long time coming." After an emotional several minutes of sobbing and wiping each other's eyes, Sarai and Hagar kissed each other; Hagar returned to her seat and Sarai continued with her story.

It all began, Sarai said, when my husband Abram told me of his strange experience with our God one evening when God said Abram should leave his father's house, his country and family and go somewhere. Since somewhere was not a clear destination, Abram was perplexed as to where it was he should go. The *going* was a puzzling command because God did not say where Abram should go, He just told Abram He would show him. Show him what, show him where, I pondered in my mind? But because my husband was an obedient man, he proceeded to make preparations to go wherever he thought God would tell him to go. Yet and still, it was the promise that followed the instruction to go which so completely confused my husband and myself. God told my husband that a great nation would come out from him. Further, God spoke these words to Abram, "*And I will make of thee a great nation, and I will bless thee, and make thy name great; and thou shalt be a blessing: and in thee shall all families of the earth be blessed.*" All families of the earth I questioned? What does that mean I asked Abram? Sarai said she reminded Abram that he was 75-years old and no children had been born from them, so where was this great nation to come from? Neither of us she continued, had an answer to our question of God, and He was not forthcoming with any explanations beyond what He had already said. So, my husband Abram took me, our possessions, our cattle, our servants, all that we owned, and Abram's nephew Lot with all of his possessions, and we left Haran and set out for somewhere. The direction that we took was toward the land of Canaan. As we traveled into Canaan, then onto other lands, and on into Egypt, God continued to remind Abram of His promise that a great nation would come from him.

At this point in her story, Sarai turned to Lot's wife and said, it was during those times as you have so beautifully described, that your husband Lot, my husband's nephew parted from his uncle. And you are right. It was a very sad time for them both because of the love they each had for one another. Also, it took quite some time for our people in our camp to get over the loss of Lot and his separation from us. But we continued on.

After some years, the subject of great nations coming out of Abram surfaced again. Inwardly I had hoped this was a discussion no longer worthy of repeating or even thinking about because so many years had passed since God had spoken this promise to Abram. I had determined that maybe my Abram had not heard God as clearly as he first thought. He was old and so was I and we still had brought forth not one child. But, here it was again, this subject of children from Abram. And the more I thought about it the closer I came to what I believed to be the solution to the problem as I understood it to be. Since I was too old to bear children but my handmaiden was still of child-bearing age, I would simply have her conceive of Abram's seed and bring forth the child. In that way the child would belong to me, since everything the handmaiden owned was really not hers at all but mine, because even she was mine. At that point in her story, Sarai realizing what she had just said, looked over at Hagar with a look of apology and Hagar returned her look with an understanding nod and a reassuring expression.

Feeling encouraged by Hagar, Sarai continued. So, I told Abram of my thoughts about God's promise that perhaps the promise would come through Hagar instead of me. I told him to go in to Hagar's tent and allow her to receive his seed. I must admit now that I was somewhat disturbed that he did not protest, nor insist that God's promise meant children between the two of us instead of him and my handmaiden. He simply did as I asked without offering any objection or complaint. At that exact moment, I regretted my decision but was too proud to withdraw it. And that was the beginning of my resentment for my dear handmaiden Hagar. Our relationship became adversarial from then on and it was through no fault of hers, but purely mine. You see, we all must reap the aftermath of our decisions and behaviors, and I have regretted my hasty and foolish decision many times over. I don't know why I felt the need to interfere with God's plan or act as though He needed my help to move it along in order for it to come to pass. But alas I did.

Well, it wasn't very long after Hagar and my husband had come together a number of times that Hagar knew she was with child. Then looking over at Hagar, Sarai said, "You were never so eager to come into my presence and find reasons to tend to me than when you were in your childbearing condition Hagar." With a sheepish smile, Hagar nodded as did Sarai, as though the two of them had a very intimate connection with one another. Sarai proceeded with her story. I was quite displeased with myself because of the outcome that resulted from my interference with God's plan. So in my anger I pressed Hagar harder than what was reasonable and fair. And it was my pressing and increased cruelty that caused her to run away from us and into the desert alone. But shortly after running away, she returned, and I had unsettled feelings about her return. I was glad she was back within the safety of our camp instead of alone and unprotected in the desert for any man to terrorize. But I was also unhappy about having to see her every day in her childbearing condition as an open reminder to me of my inability to bear children.

Soon thereafter, my 86-year-old husband was given a son brought forth by another woman, my handmaiden Hagar. Ishmael was the name given to their son because she said that's the name God told her to give him when she was alone in the desert. So here we were, 11-years after God's first promise to Abram that he would become the father of many nations, and thus far Abram's nations consisted of just this one son. But I must remember not to protest too strongly against our God because He has always been faithful to us. Also, I must admit here and now that there always remained a small amount of hope within me that God's promise of nations from Abram would include me. And even though I was old and well beyond my child-bearing age, I wanted to be the one through whom these nations would come. If my husband Abram was to be the father of nations, I wanted to be the mother of nations by way of my own loins and not the loins of another. That was my secret hope all those years which I shared with no one, and now, I share it with all of you for the first time. Immediately as if on cue, all the women rushed to Sarai's side and embraced her. They all seemed to understand her pain of the moment.

As Sarai continued with her story she acknowledged the pleasantness of her life. We had a good life, she said. Abram was well respected among the other nations of people we encountered in our travels across the beautiful desert that was our countryside. And because I was his wife, I was treated with great respect; and I don't mind confessing that I enjoyed this good life of ours. We had everything we needed and lacked nothing. Our servants were also well cared for,

129

respected, and even envied among the servant populations of other nations of people. There were many, many children among us and Ishmael reigned as the favorite because of who his father was. No one questioned my husband Abram about any of his decisions. His army was well trained in combat and strategy and obeyed him without question, even when he commanded them to be circumcised along with all the other men in the camp.

When Abram was 99-years old, our God appeared before him again with the same age-old promise of nations. I was beginning to get weary of this promise that kept coming but which yielded no results. I was still barren! This time however, the promise included a name change for me and my husband. God changed Abram's name to Abraham and my name from Sarai to Sarah. The promise also distinctly identified me as the mother of Abraham's descendants. God said, *"I will bless her, and you will have a son by her. She will become the mother of nations, and some of her descendants will even be kings."* I was beside myself with joy when Abraham told me of God's promise this time.

Then one very hot day during the warm season of the year, my lord and husband Abraham was sitting in his usual place at the opening of the tent enjoying the infrequent yet welcomed breezes that periodically crossed the threshold of our tent. I was further back in the interior of our tent when I heard the still quietness of the day abruptly broken by the utterances of my husband in conversation with the voices of men that were completely unfamiliar to me. I looked to see who had approached our tent so quietly, for I had not heard the approaching of camels, or donkeys or wagons, just the suddenness of voices in conversation. When I looked, I saw that three men, complete strangers to me had unexpectedly appeared to my lord. After greeting them with much respect, my husband quickly sent for water for them to wash their feet. After which he told me to prepare a meal and ordered our servants to prepare one of our best young calves for the strangers as they must assuredly be hungry after having traveled from wherever they had come. Milk, curds, and the roasted calf were all prepared with great detail and served to the men seated under the shade of the tree outside our tent as my husband Abraham stood in quiet respect allowing the men to consume their meal in peace. It was only after they invited him to join them that Abraham sat to partake of the meal with his guests. After a while one of the visitors asked Abraham of my whereabouts. I could hear them very clearly because I stood near enough to the opening of our tent to allow my ears to hear their every word, yet far enough behind the folds of the opening so I would not be visible to them even if they looked in the direction of the tent opening. So, in response to their inquiry, Abraham told them I was in the tent. As they continued to speak, once again, the promise of nations from Abraham was mentioned by one of the men. I couldn't believe my ears when I heard what came next from the mouth of one of the men who said, "*I will certainly return unto thee according to the time of life; about this time next year, and, lo, Sarah thy wife shall have a son.*" Was I dreaming? This time the promise actually had a time frame attached to it. It was very clear and distinct. Here we were in our old age, and it was finally going to happen that Abraham and I would once again know the tender happiness of coming together, and that we would produce a son. Was the promise here at last? I was so excited, all I could do was laugh in utter excitement and much joy. But quickly I covered my mouth as I realized my laugh had been heard. Then the man who spoke the promise, asked Abraham, "*Why did Sarah laugh? Does she doubt that she can have a child in her old age? I am the LORD! There is nothing too difficult for me. I'll come back next year at the time I promised, and Sarah will already have a son.*" I was so frightened by His words and by the fact that he heard me laugh, that instinctively I lied and said I had not laughed. But it was too late, he had heard me laugh, "*Yes, you did!*" he responded. Suddenly the joy I first felt at hearing the exactness of the date for my son's birth, turned to sheer fright. Had my laughter and my lie placed the promise in danger of not happening because of my reaction? I was deeply troubled and sat down at the other end of the tent away from the opening. I just sat there in a troubled daze for so long that I did not hear the men when they bade Abraham farewell and left. Then as I continued to sit in saddened spirit, I felt the unexpected presence of my husband Abraham as he came to me with open arms to comfort me as if he knew exactly what I was feeling. My joy began to return as I sat with Abraham in his arms and we offered no words between us because none were necessary.

Within days after the men had visited us, a renewed tenderness arose between Abraham and myself. When he came in to my tent during the times of our coming together after the promise, those times were—how shall I say it—they were absolutely wonderful. They were far more tantalizing and exciting than they had ever been for many years. He was as if he was a much younger man, and I was…Ohhh my! Here Sarah lifted a corner of her robe and began to fan herself; she then glanced over to Hagar and they gave each other a knowing look and a sheepish smile. The rest of the women giggled softly, some covering their mouths as if to hide their smiles. Then after more fanning, Sarah gained her composure to continue her story. While all this non-verbal communication was going on between the women in the room over the subject of Abraham, Jennifer had a few mental flash-backs of the times she had read or heard the story in Genesis preached of Sarah's pregnancy and ultimate delivery of her son Isaac. Jennifer, on those occasions had cringed at the very notion of engaging in sexual intercourse with a 99-year old man. The very thought of such lovemaking had sometimes made her almost gag. Therefore, it was during those moments that she reverted to simply accepting the scriptural text as it was written without delving into the reality of the passage as an actual lived experience. She had reasoned that some of the narratives carried far too much emotion for her to try and imagine what the experience might have really been like. And this account was one such case in regard to her reflections on sexual intimacy with 99-year-old Abraham. But here, now, in her own home with Sarah and Hagar blushing and the rest of the women reacting the way they were at the mention of Abraham's 99-year old sexual prowess, Jennifer came to a realization. Everything Scriptural should not and could not be measured according to the standards of 21st century linguistics, upbringing, and reasoning. The very unique way that Sarah and the other women referred to "love making" as "coming together" brought clarity to that fact.

Sarah continued with her account of the manner in which God had miraculously transformed her and Abraham's coming together with the pleasure and intimacy that had once been theirs when they were much younger. But it had all returned with a seemingly increased intensity and enjoyment. Sarah could barely contain herself as she told her story and the women were all locked into her account of what had happened between her and Abraham as if they too were experiencing exactly what Sarah was describing. Jennifer lightly chucked to herself at the sight of their uniform reaction which was so fixed on Sarah that not one of them even noticed Jennifer's amusement. As Sarah continued, she admitted that she had been so anxious to receive God's promise of bearing a son that she had completely forgotten all about the physical changes that accompanied childbearing and more specifically, what those changes would look like and feel like for the body of an 89-year old woman. But she was completely surprised and totally grateful to her God that her aged body managed the child-bearing changes very well. Then looking around the room, she asked, "Is anything too hard for our God?" In unison, everyone shook their heads, "No!" they all responded. Continuing, Sarah said she had actually felt young again, not only in her body but in her mind and in her spirit. What a wonderful experience this child-bearing turned out to be. She walked with pride throughout the camp and held her head high because she could now fully understand her part in God's amazing promise; and she was proud to bear the visible evidence of that incredible promise. Indeed, people as numerous as the stars in the heavens and the grains of sand on the shores would come from her; and she would become forever known as the mother of nations and kings and nobles. How wonderful!

Basking in all of this wonderment, Sarah said she was suddenly struck with a reminder that her time to deliver had come at the exact time of year that the men who visited Abraham had said it would be. I was thrilled beyond words, she continued, when my time came for me to bring forth my son. Despite the pain of delivering Abraham's man-child from my own loins, I wanted to hold on to the memory of that experience for as long as I could possibly bear it, Sarah said. I was also comforted by my very able mid-wives who were with me and attentive to my every need as I reveled in the coming forth of new life. Then turning to Hannah, Sarah said, my dear sister, I know you can understand and share the unspeakable joy I felt at being no longer barren, since you and I both shared that awful dishonor until our beneficent God intervened for us by opening our wombs. Hannah smiled knowingly and shook her head in agreement with

Sarah's testimonial. Sarah continued, when I held my precious little son in my arms for the first time after his birth I could scarcely believe my own eyes. All I could think was, he came from me and not another, he came from me. My joy could have filled the entire world many times over especially when I saw the look on my husband Abraham's face who was 100-years old by then when he looked upon our beautiful son for the first time and then looked at me with such love in his eyes. I was 90-years old, and my husband had made me laugh and had brought such joy and delight into my life. Had I died at that moment, I would have been content.

Abraham named our son Isaac and took him when he was only 8-days old from my breast long enough to circumcise him. And because of my son's distress at his circumcision, I nursed him immediately after the circumcision to sooth him and comfort him from that painful ordeal. I derived such pleasure and comfort from nursing my son, of caring for him, of holding him in my arms, and watching every little measure of progress he made day-by-day. The first little sounds he made as he attempted to speak to me in his little baby language were like musical notes to my ears. The softness and tenderness of his voice thrilled me beyond my ability to put into words right now. As Sarah recalled Isaac's young life her face brightened and her eyes took on the typically glazed over look of immeasurable love that mothers display when reminiscing about their children. It was a countenance of Mother's love, and all the women in the room seemed to immediately go to that similar place in their own memories as they listened to Sarah's account of little Isaac's growing up years. Jennifer was not a mother so she could not share the look or feel the emotion these women were experiencing. But she could very easily recall the countless times she had seen that same expression on her own mother's face whenever she recounted some of the youthful behaviors Jennifer or her siblings demonstrated. This must be one of those "mother's moments" Jennifer thought realizing that she would not completely understand that kind of love until she herself became a mother.

Sarah continued on. None of my other duties as the primary woman within our camp, as the wife of Abraham mattered to me very much while my Isaac was young. I was so delighted that finally I had born a child that all other things became quite unimportant. Here I was, a 90-year old woman who had just given birth to her first baby, and was able to nurse him at the breast, imagine that! Sarah was almost giddy. Isaac and his care and attention occupied my every moment except the times his father Abraham and I came together. I often wondered if God would grant me another child to contribute to the nations that He said were to come from Abraham and me. But Isaac was my only child. After all, God had promised us a son and had kept His word, and so I was satisfied. I was very happy indeed with Isaac. He continued to grow fast and strong until the time of weaning and I had to release him from that part of our mother-son bonding. He seemed to tolerate the separation much easier than I did. His father held a great feast for the occasion of his son Isaac's weaning and there was much celebrating throughout the camp for the observance of the weaning. Isaac quickly wasted no time spending much more time frolicking with the other boys in the camp and especially his half-brother Ishmael. He also began spending more time with his father as though he was trying very hard to become a man. My little Isaac was indeed becoming a man, Sarah chuckled.

As I watched him one day with his brother Ishmael, I noticed that yet again, Ishmael seemed a little too harsh with my Isaac, and it was not the first time I had seen such rough play and bitter teasing. Isaac didn't seem to mind, in fact he seemed to enjoy the roughness of his elder brother's attention. But I was not so good-natured about it. Even though Isaac didn't seem to mind, I did, and I had had enough. I went to Abraham to complain and tell him what Ishmael was doing. I was so upset that I told Abraham Ishmael and his mother must no longer remain with us, but should be made to leave our camp. Abraham was sorely disappointed and saddened by my request to rid our camp of Ishmael and his mother, but since his pattern was to deny me almost none of my requests, he gave in to this one as well.

And even though I believe this request of mine was the one most grievous to him ever, he still complied with my desire. At this point in her narrative, Sarah again turned to Hagar with an apologetic glance. And again, Hagar seemed to understand, and imparted to Sarah a go-ahead nod. Noticing the frequent back and forth glances between Sarah and Hagar and the emotions integral to their relationship, Jennifer gained a greater insight into the courageous and wonderful tenacity of these women who were with her to tell their stories. She realized that no matter how difficult or painful the stories were; they must be told from the mouths and experiences of the ones who had lived through the sufferings.

Sarah continued speaking. As the years passed and my beloved and precious son grew into such strong and highly favored manhood, he began to spend much more time with his father, going almost everywhere with him. I derived much pleasure from seeing them together doing the things that men enjoy doing, especially because it made my husband so very happy during those times together with the son I bore him. My precious Isaac was the son who took away my shame of barrenness. But there was one time that I became so distressed and filled with anguish and misery that

I nearly collapsed in such a tormented state, I thought I would absolutely never recover. My husband took our son on a typical journey to offer sacrifices to our God which was not unusual in the least. In fact, it was quite common. But what occurred during that particular trip nearly destroyed me for good. With a few servants, some daily supplies, along with the sacrifice fire and wood, my husband and Isaac set off into the desert. After reaching a set location, Abraham took our son up to a high location on the mountain while leaving the servants behind. Once reaching the place of sacrifice, Abraham made the altar ready for the sacrifice with the wood and the fire. But because he had such a sharp mind, Isaac inquired of his father concerning the whereabouts of the lamb for sacrifice seeing that the altar was in order, the wood was in place and the fire was ready. Abraham responded that the Lord would provide the sacrifice. He then placed our son Isaac upon the altar, bound his hands and feet, drew out his dagger and raising it high into the air, prepared to actually kill our son upon the altar of sacrifice. I can only imagine the sheer heart-pounding fright that my Isaac must have felt during those frightful moments that he lay helplessly bound on the altar watching his father with his dagger in hand, his arm raised high in the air in preparation for the one plunging swing of his arm straight into his heart. At this moment in her storyline, Sarah drew in a deep, long breath as if attempting to steady herself from losing her breath altogether. And with great concern, everyone, including Jennifer leaned forward as if to assist Sarah in her breathing. They could see her pain. After several tense moments Sarah was able to regain her strength and proceeded to share her history. Sarah spoke this time with haltering voice as she said, it was at that most crucial instance when my son's life was rushing headlong into death that an angel of the Lord spoke out to Abraham telling him not to slay Isaac. Oh my sisters, I never quite recovered from that ordeal, not for the rest of my life. It placed somewhat of a strain between my husband Abraham and me. And although I believed him when he told me he was acting in absolute obedience to our God, I still remained troubled by it all. I am a mother, and we all know, except you Jennifer dear, the strong emotions and connections that we as mothers carry within ourselves for our children. I loved my only son so very dearly, and to have lost him that way would have completely destroyed me even unto my own death. And even now as I speak of that troubling torment, I must remind myself of the explanation our God gave me concerning it. It was not until after I had reached the realm of the dead and our God comforted me with the knowledge that He never intended for our son to be sacrificed that I could begin to understand it. And even though I would have been grateful to our God if that incident had never happened, I was and am still ever mindful of my appreciation and thankfulness to Him for permitting me to experience His great blessing of motherhood. In fact, I have never stopped thanking Him. He took me from the ranks of barren womanhood into the wonderful world of productive motherhood and I am eternally grateful.

Turning to Jennifer, Sarah commented, Jennifer my dear, I am told that the word barren is no longer used in your society as a way to identify women. Is that true? "Yes" was Jennifer's response. Also, continued Sarah, the determination to not have children seems to be a decision that the women of your time can make at will whenever they wish. Is that also true? "Yes" was Jennifer's response again. I am amazed, said Sarah, at such thinking among these 21st century women; they do not all seem to have the same anxious desires to become mothers as we had in our time. In fact I am told that some women of this era intentionally deny themselves the great pleasures and privileges of motherhood by making deliberate choices to avoid becoming mothers altogether. Am I correct in my understanding Jennifer? Jennifer nodded and replied, "Yes, you are correct in your understanding, but I am not one of those women. I plan to marry and have children." Everyone smiled.

Chapter 10
I Loved My Husband

Opening her mouth to speak, the next woman turned to Mrs. Lot and said, "I too have been maligned over the centuries and have also been known only by my husband's name. I'm simply called Job's wife. And just like you my dear wife of Lot, I have been so unfairly labeled by countless people. Many of whom have marked me as an unkind, uncaring and insensitive wife." The ache in this woman's voice was unmistakable as she spoke of the character destroying documentation in sacred text that had so unfairly defined her and desecrated her reputation as a wife. And according to her, it was all completely untrue. It seemed to her that very few had tried to understand or even consider the deep and penetrating grief she had been forced to experience. Not even her husband understood her statement to him. He thought she was being vile, wicked and stupid. "But I wasn't," she said. Continuing on, she said further that she felt such pain watching him suffer the way he did while she was completely helpless to do anything about it. She could not comfort him or ease his pain, nor put an end to the tragedies that were attacking him from seemingly every side. Thus it was her suffering anguish, not her insensitivity that prompted her to speak the words which have become more known about her than her personal pain. In reality, it was her devotion to her husband that prompted her statement. Not knowing what else to do, and based on her deep and abiding affection for her beloved husband, Job's wife imagined that death would be better and less painful for him than the agony he was experiencing. At the very least, death would remove him from his sorrowful state so that he would no longer be at the mercy or lack thereof of the torturous shredding of his body bit by bit. Job's wife confessed that she neither knew nor understood her husband's God. What kind of God she questioned in her mind, would permit such suffering to someone as dear and righteous as her upstanding Job?

Of course Mrs. Job knew nothing of the conversation that had taken place between her husband's God and her husband's enemy. That conversation was designed by Job's God to prove to Job's enemy, that Job was indeed the upright and righteous man he appeared to be and would remain so even if stripped of his good life and reduced to a mere shell of his former self. It was because of this conversation that a grueling course of events was initiated against Job in order to dispel any doubt about his blameless character. But since Mrs. Job was not aware of the conversation, she was completely unable to make sense of the fierce integrity her Job continued to maintain toward his far away God who rewarded Job's high moral character with disease and agonizing malady. As she witnessed her husband hold fast to his high regard for his God, she was mystified to understand this degree of integrity or loyalty. Hence, she suggested as gently as her voice would allow, and with all the helplessness of her being, that perhaps Job should quickly curse his God and just die. Surely the ire of her husband's God at Job's cursing would result in a swift and immediate ending of Job's life. Death she reasoned would seem more merciful and kind than the continual and unbearably painful existence that lingered upon Job with a tenacious refusal to subside or let go. She thought that if he would agree to curse his God and die, then she would die along with him and they would both be relieved of the pain that had so uprooted and devastated their lives. But there was no death to alleviate their woes. And what was even more hurtful was that Job had not grasped the meaning or intent of his wife's statement. It had seemed outlandish to him. He had not listened to her the way she wanted to be heard. He did not hear the sadness in her heart, he had not seen the tears she shed every night since the beginning of his troubles, and he had not heard her nightly sobs. Instead, he simply dismissed his wife's expression of concern and forthrightly accused her of speaking foolishly. "You speak as the foolish women speak," he reprimanded. In vain she tried to explain and defend her statement, but Job was not in his best state of mind, he would hear nothing else of what she so desperately wanted him to understand.

Proceeding with her story, Job's wife continued her account of that horrendous period in her life during which the two major components of her life had been inexplicably snatched away. Her classification and identity as a woman of distinction because she was Job's wife had been so devastatingly eroded. And the recognition and tremendous satisfaction of motherhood which had been hers to enjoy because she was the mother of 10 children had been completely wiped away. In recalling the deep tormenting emptiness which befell her after the untimely loss of all her children, Job's wife refers to that time as torturously unbearable.

All ten of my children, she recites, had been suddenly and without warning destroyed in the strangest turn of events when my eldest son's house collapsed while the rest of my children were all gathered in his house to celebrate the coming of age of my youngest son. And it was while I was in deep mourning over this tragic death of my children that just as suddenly as they had been destroyed, my husband Job began to experience the worst kind of sickness of his entire life. I wondered how much more I could possibly bear. I lived day-after-day in a state of helpless despair, not knowing how I would face the next day. And there were times when I wondered if I even cared to face the next day. After all, each day seemed to bring more of the previous day's anguish. So then, as I contemplated my life, I pondered which of these two agonies was worse. Was it the unique and specific pain and endless grief that I felt as a mother over the

145

loss of my children or was it the tragic and hurtful accusation of my husband whose indictment against me was that I had behaved like one of the foolish village women? Did he not remember how much I loved him? Was he so quick to forget how I labored over the boiling pots to mix and combine herbs and spices in an effort to concoct soothing balms and ointments for his sores? Had he not given thought of how I prepared the purest of linens and finest silks for use as wrapping cloths to place on his infested body? And through all of this I still felt the helplessness of being unable to make the slightest difference or improvement in my Job's miserable condition. There were times I thought I would simply burst. I had been forced to endure this anguish without so much as a glimmer of hope that the excruciating and odoriferous state of my husband's sickness would ever cease. Then, at this point in her recollection, Job's wife completely broke down into a sobbing heap as the women swiftly gathered around her to offer comfort.

Gaining some composure, Job's wife continued. And what of my children? I felt lost without them. Their absence left an enormous gaping chasm in my very soul that could not be filled. How could I survive without the comfort and company of my children all of whom had grown into such wonderful and caring young men and young women? I found myself longing for the former days of the break-of-day rituals of gathering wood for the early morning fire to prepare the first meal of the day. That had been such an enjoyable time for the family when we all drew together in preparation for the day's events which lay before us. But precious little time was being given now to food preparation and pleasant mealtimes; neither I nor my husband had much desire for food. Job was losing his appetite as well as his weight. And now, my days were filled with the repetitive chores of wrapping and re-wrapping my husband's wounds and sores. But even with my deliberate attention and attempts at curative remedies, my Job's wounds and sores were still no closer to healing than they had ever been, in fact they were getting increasingly worse. I somehow began to feel a sense of blame for my husband's wretched state of existence. What had I done? Had I unknowingly done or said something wrong or offensive to or about my husband's God and was this the punishment He had meted out to me? I also admit to having felt that same nagging self-reproach about the loss of my children all of whom had been so swiftly snatched away from me in the blink-of-an-eye. If only I could remember what I had done or said, then I could have quickly repented and pleaded for forgiveness to perhaps bring about a reversal of all that had befallen my family. But my memory would not recall anything I had done to bring about this calamity, nor did my memory bring to the surface any forbidden statement I might have made that would be responsible for this life-altering misfortune. And so it was, that night after night I cried myself to sleep contemplating how my children must have suffered a slow and excruciating death buried beneath the heavy and massive rubble of the collapsed house which had previously been my son's beautiful home.

I wanted desperately to die. One gloom-filled night, as I lay awake tormented by the memories of my children and the life I used to live when they were alive, I intentionally and with as much ferocity as I could muster, loudly and forcefully cursed my husband's God on my own behalf. It was my hope that this God who received such allegiance and respect from my husband would instantly kill me right where I lay for the audacity of my disrespect. But alas, He did not. I remained quite alive only to continue lingering in a living state of unhappy misery.

Forced to continue life in this most appalling manner I even lessened my trips to the marketplace because I could barely stand to hear the whispers and taunts of the people or endure their glares of disdain; or the way they moved away from me when they saw me approaching. Many times I witnessed some of the younger men who had not even gained the respect of the village nor the recognition of the elders, now berating my husband with their unruly jeers and boisterous song-like taunts. How dare these immature, societal cast-offs exercise their unlearned impudence to speak so contemptuously of my formerly well respected and upright husband. How dare they indeed! At this point in her tirade, Job's wife was standing and pacing the floor and stamping her feet and waving her arms with emotional outrage. How dare they, she shouted, again and again, how dare they! The women all sat quietly in deep understanding concern, allowing her to release her frustration and indignation. They began whispering that she had probably been holding in all this rage for millennia, and now was as good a time as ever to let it out. A few of them even joined in with her, yes indeed my dear, how dare they speak so rudely of your Job, after all, he was a man of upright standing who shunned evil. After a few more moments of communal voice-raising and waving of the arms, things settled down and Job's wife looked around at her sisters-in-life, lowered her head and covered her face with her hands. Oh my sisters, she said, I am so sorry, we are supposed to be sharing our stories with Jennifer and here I am ranting like a foolish woman indeed. Oh no, no, the women responded sympathetically, you have been deeply wounded and Jennifer understands, don't you dear? Jennifer with open mouth, simply nodded.

Moving on with her story, Job's wife said, our family had alienated themselves from us, our friends who had often joined us for celebrations and feasts began to shun and avoid us. They acted as if they never knew us. People who once proclaimed their undying love and respect for us and whom we also loved, turned their backs on us. Even our servants behaved in a disrespectful manner toward my husband. And all the while, my poor ailing husband bore the appearance of a collection of walking bones covered only with skin. I even once heard him say that he had escaped only by the skin of his teeth.

There was a time when three of my husband's closest friends came to visit him because they thought they could somehow help him see the error of his ways which in keeping with their thoughts was the cause of his troubles. They sat with my husband for days and days talking and accusing, and talking some more about the reasons for my husband's condition and the apparent iniquitous relationship he had with his God. And although my husband cursed the day of his birth stating he would have been better off dying on the day of his birth rather than living to the place in life where he now found himself, I overhead him say one day that he was waiting until his change came. What a confusing paradox. Wanting to die one minute yet all the while declaring and waiting for a forthcoming change. What change was he waiting for? I could not understand his reasoning which seemed surely to be rooted in something other than human logic.

But one day as my husband was yet again ruing the day he had been born, his God appeared to him finally after so long a time of absolute silence. He began speaking to Job in a scolding manner and questioning him of his whereabouts when the earth was being formed, and when the skies rage with lightning and thunder, and many other matters which are entirely out of the realm of human control. My husband found himself completely incapable of responding to God's interrogations, and he repented of his former doubtful comments and accusations of God. Then, it was only after my husband's repentance and declaration that he now knew God firsthand and more intimately than formerly knowing Him only through words of hearsay from others, that God's scathing monologue ceased. God then turned His anger toward my husband's friends, Eliphaz the Temanite, Bildad the Shuhite and Zophar the Naamathite telling them of His displeasure at their manner of speaking to Job and further that they should offer a sacrifice in Job's presence so that Job could pray for them. After my husband's prayer for them, an amazing transformation unfolded. God began to heal Job of his decaying sores. God even began to bless Job all over again as in our former days. Miraculously, all of our fortunes, treasures, livestock, and everything we had previously possessed materialized again back into our lives twice as abundant as before Job's sickness. Our family and friends returned to us, and even brought us gifts of gold and silver.

Then, at this point in her story, Job's wife covered her face again and blushed as she recounted that she and her husband even had more children, seven sons and three beautiful daughters. Still blushing, she said, it was not only my husband's material possessions which became twice as abundant, but his vigor in the way he touched and loved me became twice as intense as he had previously been. It seemed as if he had again become young and full of the former vitality that had so enthralled me in our youthful days whenever we came together. Here, Mrs. Job ceased her narrative and simply stared off into space as if she was revisiting and reliving a most wonderful and exciting time in her life. After a few moments, she slightly shivered, blinked her eyes as if emerging from a trance, and looked around the room at the rest of the women as though she had just returned from a very faraway place. And it was at this point that each of the other women were all smiling, some with closed eyes, as if they too had just experienced a few moments of a similar warm and tender reminiscence.

Composed once again, Mrs. Job resumed her story. In addition to being an upright man, my Job was also more progressive in his thinking about the practices of inheritance transference than was customary during that time. He saw to it that our new daughters were given the same rights to inherit property, goods, and all other personal possessions belonging to Job upon his death in equal value and amounts as our new sons were given in accordance to the customs of our time.

It was in the shadows of and after the recovery from Job's harrowing ordeal and for many, many years after, that he and I lived long and prosperous lives in the same bountiful manner as we had previously lived before his debilitating sickness nearly destroyed him. Thus well into our old age, our latter years were filled with riches, honor, and abundance, along with the magnificent pleasure we enjoyed because of and through our new children, and their children, and their children's children. And just as he did before his sickness with our first set of children when he sought God on their behalf; my Job resumed his practice of praying to God for our new children. He did so with the same intent to seek forgiveness and absolution on their behalf in the event they had inadvertently or willfully sinned before God. Also in those latter years, Job's God very tenderly and lovingly appeared before me, comforted me and invited me to know Him as Job knew Him. In eagerness I opened my heart and mind and readily learned who this God really was; I embraced Him as my own God and loved Him dearly. Then

I too had a deeply abiding love for the same God that Job had always loved and whom I now loved. I was finally able to understand Job's profound devotion to Him which made it easier for me to develop my own personal relationship with Him. Therefore, whenever my husband prayed for our children as he had in the former years, I also prayed for our children right there alongside my Job. And even though I never stopped aching from the loss of my children destroyed in the earlier catastrophe and wistfully longed for their presence, my perfect and wonderful God understood that in my new joy there still resided some old pain. He comforted me through those moments.

Chapter 11
Messiah My Son

Jennifer my dear you have been so patient with us, I hope we have not tired you with our stories. But I must tell you my story and then we will leave you to get your rest. My name is Mary. Some call me Mother Mary, some call me Virgin Mary, some call me Madonna, some even call me Blessed Virgin, but the name my father gave me was simply Mary. I grew up in a loving home with my 5 brothers and 4 sisters, and was the youngest of my parents 10 children. After my brothers and elder sisters had married and gone out of my parent's home to live their lives with their own growing families, I remained alone in my parents' home. I felt quite lonely then, especially after my sister just above me in age had married and moved away and into her husband's family.

Living in the small village of Nazareth which was situated in the larger city of Galilee, it wasn't long after my sister married, that my parents decided it was time for me to marry also. So they met again with the parents in our village with whom they had previously made arrangements when I was a child, that I would marry their young son Joseph when he and I both became of age. The time had come, according to our parents, and it was discussed among them and agreed upon that Joseph and I were both old enough and that now was the appropriate time for me to become betrothed to him for marriage. Neither Joseph nor I had ever been consulted in the matter, but we both knew according to our customs that the subject was settled in keeping with our parent's decision. So, at a young age I was engaged to marry Joseph, a direct descendent from the house of King David.

One mid-morning, as I sat pondering marriage and what all that would entail, I was startled by the sudden presence of a man who introduced himself as Gabriel. He greeted me by name and told me I was highly favored of God and that the

Lord was with me. I was too frightened to speak and certainly very perplexed by his presence, what he was saying, what he meant and most of all why he had come. Hearing him tell me how favored I was in the sight of our God was completely shocking to me since I was just a woman. In our tradition, it was the men who were favored by God and who received visitations from strange and wonderful beings claiming to be messengers of God. I could not understand how I, a mere woman was being visited by and spoken to directly face-to-face instead of through a male authority figure in my life. It was quite perplexing indeed. This was clearly not the practice of my people or any other people of that time for that matter. A man engaging in public conversation with a woman without the presence and or permission of another male authority or elder relative, was unspeakable. Yet, here it was happening to me with a man I had never seen before and who had actually seemed to respect me enough to identify himself to me by name, Gabriel. He showed not even the slightest concern for our convention of male, female verbal interaction and continued speaking to me as though it was completely proper and quite in order. Sensing my fear and bewilderment, he tried to comfort me by telling me not to be afraid and repeated his claim that I had found favor with God. But his attempt at comfort held very little influence when his conversation swiftly took a most audacious and bizarre turn. He said I would very soon conceive and bear a son. Now it seemed he was being presumptuous and intimate beyond his right to be so. Certainly it was my hope to one day conceive after Joseph and I married, but hearing such detailed intimacy from the lips of another man before Joseph and I had even spoken of such things, was frightening to me and seemingly impudent on his part, especially when he went so far as to name my son for me and tell me that he would be great, all the while detailing his future and purpose in life. I must admit that the notion of my son being great was flattering to me. But Gabriel didn't stop there, he made the most outrageous claims that my son would be known as the son of the Most High, that the Lord would give him the throne of Father David, that he would forever reign over the house of Father Jacob and that there would be no end to his kingdom. I soon began to tremble and wanted to run away from this brazen man whom I did not know; he was speaking blasphemy and I felt I would be punished for remaining in his presence while he spoke such things. But, I could not move. My lips quivered as I tried to speak, and what emerged from my mouth was a barely audible whisper as I told Gabriel that I had not yet married Joseph and was still a virgin, therefore these things that he was speaking simply could not be so. Then my heart nearly stopped beating in my bosom when he said he knew I was a virgin and for that reason it would be the Holy Spirit who would come upon me and the Most High would overshadow me and the child would be called Holy, the son of God. I covered my ears then clutched my heart; how could he speak of our Most High God of all Israel in such a manner. Who was this brash man named Gabriel and why had not God struck him dead right where he stood? I could not bear to listen any longer, I fainted right off of my seat, right there on the spot.

As I opened my eyes, I thought I would find that Gabriel was no longer present and I would realize I had experienced a most peculiar and absurd dream. But, when I opened my eyes, there was Gabriel, still where he was when I fainted. He had protected me from injuring myself in my fall and helped me back into my sitting position when I awakened from my faint. He resumed his conversation as though nothing unusual had happened telling me further that my cousin Elizabeth who had been barren was now with child as far along as six months despite her old age; and that she too would also give birth to a son. Well, after hearing what he had said about me, I was not the least bit alarmed at his news concerning Elizabeth. Still trying to help me comprehend all that he had spoken he assured me that nothing is impossible with God. I certainly could not dispute that fact in light of the countless stories of God's interventions, deliverances and miracles in the lives and conditions of our ancestors. Besides, I was too weak and still too faint to challenge Gabriel's assertions; I determined that only the continuation of time would reveal his accuracy. I had barely enough strength within me to say to Gabriel that as a servant of our Lord, I was resigned to let everything be as he had told me it would be. So I bowed my head and spoke very softly these words, "be it unto me according to thy word." And when I raised my head to look for an acknowledgement from him that he had heard my yielding to his unbelievable promises, he was no longer present. With the same suddenness as he had presented himself, he had left. I sat there unclear about what to do next. It was certain I could tell no one of what had just taken place.

But then I remembered the man Gabriel had spoken of Elizabeth; he said she in her old age was with child. I determined I must visit her to see for myself if Elizabeth was truly in the condition Gabriel had declared. But what reason could I give Elizabeth for my visit? How could I display such unkind disrespect to her by inquiring if she was with child at her age? Certainly we were all quite familiar with the account in our history of Mother Sarah having given birth to Father Isaac in her very old age, but there was nothing in our history telling us to expect another such miracle, although nothing is impossible with our God. At that moment Mary looked over at Sarah and they both smiled at each other, Sarah nodding in understanding of Mary's dilemma. I can understand completely Mary how you must have felt, Sarah said, but at least you didn't laugh in disbelief, that was my mistake. All the women chuckled softly at that statement; then Sarah spoke encouragingly to Mary, go on with your story Dear.

I wish Elizabeth had come with us tonight, Mary continued; she and I could have shared our stories together, but she is on another assignment so I will go on without her. When I arrived at her home, I needed not be concerned any longer about Elizabeth, she was plainly with child. When she saw me she received me as if she had been expecting me. And when I greeted her she placed her hand on herself and said her babe had just leaped within her for sheer joy as soon as I began to speak. Then Elizabeth was immediately filled with the Holy Spirit and asked me why the mother of her Lord had so favored her with a personal visit. She was actually referring to me as the mother of her Lord as though she already knew I was with child. But how could she have known I wondered, I had not even begun to share my story of my visit from Gabriel. She then began pronouncing blessings upon me saying that I was blessed among women, that I was blessed because I believed what I had been told would happen with me, and further that the fruit of my womb was even blessed. I was completely humbled indeed and mystified by this experience with my cousin and was uncertain what to do or say next. But somehow I recovered my voice and began to sing a song of praise to our God. My sisters, if you don't mind, I will sing it for you now. *"My soul magnifies the Lord, and my spirit rejoices in God my Savior for He has looked with favor on the lowliness of His servant. Surely, from now on all generations will call me blessed; for the Mighty One has done great things for me, and holy is His name. His mercy is for those who fear Him from generation to generation. He has shown strength with his arm; He has scattered the proud in the thoughts of their hearts. He has brought down the powerful from their thrones, and lifted up the lowly; He has filled the hungry with good things, and sent the rich away empty. He has helped his servant Israel, in remembrance of his mercy, according to the promise he made to our ancestors, to Abraham and to his descendants forever."* As Mary sang, the women in the room began to gently sway in full knowledge of the musical rhythm and melody. What a beautiful song of praise to our God, Eve said. And in harmonic unison, everyone including Jennifer agreed in a melodic response to Eve's declaration, *"A beautiful song of praise to our God indeed Blessed Mary, Mother of our Lord Jesus who is the Christ the only Lord and Savior of the world."* There was a hushed stillness in the room for a few solemn moments as everyone with closed eyes, savored the instance of musical worship and praise.

Eve spoke again, please continue Mary dear your assignment here is not yet complete. So Mary began to speak again. Even though my cousin Elizabeth was aware that I was with child and that my child would be The Lord Himself, Savior of all, I needed to share with her the details of my encounter with Gabriel. But seemingly aware of my anxiousness to tell my story, Elizabeth asked if I would permit her to speak first to tell me all that had happened to her husband Zacharias. She said it might help me to know why she already knew of my situation even before her eyes fell upon me when I arrived to visit her. She went on to tell me that her husband would be unable to greet me properly because he had been struck with an inability to speak ever since his encounter with a messenger from the Lord whose name was Gabriel. Zacharias had been carrying out his priestly duties in the Temple before the Lord when Gabriel made his appearance right alongside the altar and began speaking to Zacharias about an amazing and unbelievable promise in answer to Zacharias's prayers concerning a child.

Gabriel told Zacharias that even though he and Elizabeth were both well advanced in age, a child would indeed be born to them and would be a man-child. The child was to be raised according to a very strict set of rules from the Lord. First, the child will be great in the sight of the Lord and his given name must be John. Second, he must have no strong drink or wine. Third, he would be filled with the Holy Spirit before he was born while still in Elizabeth's womb. Fourth, he will draw the hearts and minds of the people toward the coming of the promised Messiah. Completely overwhelmed and dazed, Zacharias had questioned Gabriel about those unbelievable promises, and Gabriel's response was to render Zacharias unable to speak because of his unbelief. His ability to speak would not return until the child John was born. I was not shocked or astonished at hearing that Gabriel had made an earlier earthly visit before appearing to me, Mary said. Knowing of his visit with Zacharias made it much easier for me to tell Elizabeth my story, so I told her my entire account of Gabriel's visit leaving out no detail. And because we were both quite amazed by the outlandish similarities and promises within our stories we hugged each other in support of each other after I had completed my report; then we set about making preparations for my extended 3-month visit.

When my stay with Elizabeth came to an end, we kissed each other, said good-by and I began my return journey back home to Galilee troubled in my heart about how I would explain my circumstance to my betrothed Joseph. He was such a kind man and well respected among our people, I couldn't bear the thought of shaming him with my condition. So my troubled spirit remained with me as I pondered how I would approach the subject. In my daily prayers I sought the Lord for an answer to my dilemma; how indeed could I tell Joseph that I was with child when he and I had not yet come together. What would he think when I told him that my child was not the result of having been with a man and that I was still indeed a virgin; yes still a virgin who was with child. He would never believe me; he would think I had lost all of my senses, and I could not blame him. Even more outrageous, perhaps even insulting to Joseph's intelligence and kindness, would be my explanation that it was the spirit of our God who had come over me, had entered my body and had left me to carry an unborn child to the fullness of time for his delivery into the world. And as certain as I was of my Joseph's kindness and his generous nature, I was also certain that he would never believe such a tale, especially since my condition was the kind of sensational scandal that had the ability to bring great dishonor to his reputation. I knew also that I would become the reason for an absolute disgrace upon my entire family in addition to myself.

It would be Joseph's complete right to abandon our plans for marriage under the circumstances as they were. And I would have neither cause nor justification to consider him guilty of deserting his promise to take me as his wife. So, I made the decision that I must tell him of my condition and explain the details as best as I could. Needless to say, Joseph was quite displeased at my confession of being with child. He was not at all convinced of my truthfulness when I insisted I was still a virgin. In fact the more I explained, the more his countenance changed from utter disbelief to an enraged scowl. Joseph accused me of betraying him, of disrespecting him and most of all humiliating him with my shameful behavior. He said he could not begin to imagine how I would expect him to accept such an outrageous and blasphemous untruth. He said, aside from everything he had already said about the matter, he just could not understand how or why I wanted to hurt him with such a far reaching fable which would not remain a private matter much longer, but would soon become public knowledge for all the world to know and see. I attempted to defend myself further but at this point he turned his back to me and simply forbade me from saying anything more on the subject by demanding that I immediately cease speaking completely. Of course I obeyed him, I ceased to speak any further about it. He stood with his back to me for what seemed like an eternity. After several agonizing moments, with his back still turned, he said he was going to send me away privately from our community until the child was born so I would not have to bear the embarrassing indignity that my actions so justly deserved. He said that before the sun rose on the morrow, he would send two of his servants, a handmaiden, and a midwife along with travel provisions for my journey. He said that from this moment, I was not to speak to him or attempt to see him ever again. And without turning to face me, he walked away leaving me standing alone with a broken and aching heart. Here at this point, I was hurt and completely bewildered. Would the Most Holy Spirit of God overshadow me to make me conceive and then disgrace me at the same time in the eyes of my intended husband? I had no answers to my own questions. I made my way home and refused to eat or mingle in conversation with my family. I feigned loss of appetite and went straight into solitude to await the morning fate that my betrothed had pronounced on me.

When the morning light had dispelled the darkness of the previous night and I awoke to see a brand new day, my heart became even heavier when I heard the knock at our door; the knock I had been dreading throughout my restless night. Not wanting to disobey Joseph's demand that I look not upon his face ever again, I sat silently in my room expecting my mother to come and inform me that the traveling companions had sent word for me to come so we could begin our journey to my place of seclusion. As I waited for my mother's voice, I heard yet another familiar voice, not my mother's but a male voice that I surely recognized. It was Joseph. Why was he there? He had forbidden me to ever see him or speak to him again. Was he there to involve my family in his dictate I wondered; more dread filled my heart at the very thought of that happening. I stood with my face away from the entrance to my room if perchance Joseph should come near my room and I in error might disobey his order that I look not upon his face. I stood frozen wondering what all this meant. I was certain of Gabriel's visitation, I was certain also of the overshadowing of the spirit of our God that I might conceive and bring forth the promised Messiah, but I was not at all certain how this would affect my future. While these thoughts and uncertainties circled in my head, I heard my Joseph's voice again, but this time without the stern and hurtful tone of our last time speaking. Instead, he called me by name with a compassion that was formerly his; yet still fearful of looking upon him, I stood without turning to face him. But then I felt the gentle touch of my Joseph's hand on my shoulder as he slowly turned me to face him. I looked down. He lifted my face to his and said, "All is well my dear Mary." Completely puzzled, I listened as he told me that while he was pondering his decision to put me away privately, he drifted into a deep sleep during which time an angel of the Lord came into his dream and told him not to be afraid to take me as his wife because the child I was carrying was indeed conceived by the Holy Spirit. These are the exact words Joseph said the angel spoke to him, "*Joseph, thou son of David, fear not to take unto thee Mary thy wife: for that which is conceived in her is of the Holy Ghost. And she shall bring forth a son, and thou shalt call his name JESUS: for he shall save his people from their sins. Now all this was done, that it might be fulfilled which was spoken of the Lord by the prophet, saying, Behold, a virgin shall be with child, and shall bring forth a son, and they shall call his name Emmanuel, which being interpreted is, God with us.*" Joseph said he awoke and realized he had been spoken to by God and that what I had previously told him was completely the truth. Suddenly, we both remembered having read those sacred writings many times before, "*Behold, a virgin shall conceive, and bear a son, and shall call his name Immanuel...*" But now those words were much more than sacred writings to be read, instead they had made their way through time to become the promise spoken of and anticipated for so very long. And miracle of all miracles, this long-awaited coming Messiah was going to come forth through me. I was that virgin; imagine that, Messiah, my son. Joseph then determined that I should come with him to be his wife as the angel of the Lord had commanded him, but that we should not come together as husband and wife until after my firstborn son, the Holy Spirit conceived one, had been born. So, I went with my betrothed Joseph, son of David, to be his wife.

Joseph and I lived quietly as husband and wife. He was a good husband, attentive to my needs as a mother-to-be, and caring about our lives together. But just when I was a short period away from my time to deliver, Emperor Caesar Augustus issued a tax decree that everyone should return back to the original town where they had been born to register as the original citizens of that country and then to be taxed accordingly. As good citizens, Joseph and I left the city of Galilee where we lived and began our journey back to Bethlehem because Bethlehem was the city of David and since Joseph was a descendant of David, our obligation was to return there. It wasn't long after arriving in Bethlehem that my birth pangs began, making me know my delivery was eminent even though we had not yet reached our final living quarters in Bethlehem as we were still travelling with quite a distance yet to go. But my birth pains were coming so close together and so quickly that I realized it would be in a very

166

short time that I would give birth. When Joseph realized just how close to delivery I was, he made several attempts to find lodging for us at every travelers inn along the way. But nothing was available. People were everywhere, they were travelling in and out of the nearby towns and countries on their way to their original cities, so all the inns were full to capacity. Finally, because my delivery was forthcoming whether we found a room or not, Joseph accepted the offer of an inn keeper to use his animal stable as my birthing room to bring forth my son. And so, without the assistance of a midwife or handmaiden I gave birth right there in Bethlehem of Judea, the exact place where it was foretold in our sacred writings. But then with nowhere to lay my son, Jesus the Messiah, I used the only thing available to me which was a trough, the feeding manger for the animals in the stable. Joseph lined the manger with dry hay and straw and I wrapped and cushioned our son in soft swaddling cloths and placed him gently inside the manger. Then I laid down on the floor beside him on the additional straw and hay that Joseph had so caringly arranged for me. I was exhausted and needed rest.

I rested for what seemed like only a short time before I was awakened by a group of shepherds surrounding us and saying that a heavenly host of angels had come to the field where they were tending their sheep and had announced the birth of my child. According to the shepherds, this is what the angels told them, *"Do not be afraid; for behold, I bring you good news of great joy which will be for all the people. For this day in the city of David there has been born for you a Savior, who is Christ the Lord, the Messiah. And this will be a sign for you by which you will recognize Him: you will find a Baby wrapped in swaddling cloths and lying in a manger."* The shepherds said they had left their flocks of sheep alone in the field and had hurried quickly to find the babe who was Christ the Lord, the Messiah whom the angels spoke of. They were beside themselves with joy and excitement and even began to worship my son. Their visit however was short I'm thankful to say because they needed to return to their unattended flocks in the field. So, I lay back down in another attempt to rest from the hardship of my delivery; that's all I wanted to do. But again my rest was interrupted by another group of men coming to visit my child. I found these visits quite unusual and most interesting since it was our custom that men did not for any reason come near a woman during her time of blood every month nor during her time immediately following a delivery. But still the men continued to visit. I later understood that our customs concerning women during their time of blood were far, far less important than the birth of my son the Messiah whose coming had been foretold by the prophets of old. Now this present group of men who had just arrived were men of great wisdom from the East. They said they had come to see and worship the child who had been born king of the Jews. They knew of him because they had seen his star rising in the East and now wanted to see this king face to face to worship him and present him with the gifts of gold, frankincense, and myrrh they brought for him. They said they had been led right to us in the stable by the same star which began its rising in the East, had announced the child's birth, and then traveled in the sky above their heads leading the way to the stable where we were. After presenting their gifts to the child, they remained for a while bowing down to him, gazing at him with wonderment and worshipping him with delight and joy. They were just as excited and filled with joy as the shepherds had been.

Not long after the wise men from the East left us, my husband Joseph said we needed to leave Bethlehem and go swiftly to Egypt because he had been warned in a dream by an angel of the Lord to leave Bethlehem for the protection of the child; Herod was searching for our child to kill him. Therefore, for our very safety we left Bethlehem by the dark of night on our way to Egypt. All of this commotion surrounding my son gave me reason to recall my visit from Gabriel and wonder exactly what kind of life I would have with my son Jesus, raising him from infancy to manhood.

We had been living in Egypt for a while when we received word that Herod had died. Upon hearing this news, Joseph prepared to move us back to Judea but quickly changed his mind and sought another town when he learned that Archelaus, the son of Herod had replaced his father as ruler in Judea. So instead, Joseph made our home in the town of Nazareth. And once again, I found myself participating in the fulfillment of the words of our ancient prophet who said in reference to my son Jesus, *"He will be called a Nazarene."*

Jesus was a good child; he grew and became very strong in spirit, and was wise beyond his years. I could see the favor and grace of God upon Him. He was well adjusted and required no disciplinary actions from Joseph or me, in fact I wish I could say that about our other children, but I cannot. And working alongside his father, Jesus became quite an expert carpenter, he learned quickly and crafted extremely well. Yet and still being the mother of Jesus, the Holy One, the Savior of the world and watching him grow up was always something of a challenge. Knowing I had given birth to him, that he was my son, and that he had been conceived not by human coming together but rather by the Holy Spirit of God, I experienced a constant inner struggle between my instincts as a mother relating to her son and the knowledge that he really was not my son. There always an underlying uncertainty within me of parental authority with Jesus. Although he was always submissive to us as his parents and never disobedient, there were times when he behaved and spoke as though he was the one in authority instead of me. Let me explain further. When he was 12-years old during the time of our yearly visit to Jerusalem for the Passover Feast, we were returning home after the feast and I noticed that I had not seen Jesus for at least an entire day. We searched for him among our family caravan and realized he was nowhere to be found and no one else had seen him since we departed Jerusalem. So Joseph and I sent the other children along home with the caravan so that he and I could return to Jerusalem in search of Jesus. It was three-days before we found him. When we did find him, he was sitting in the court of the Temple among the teachers as if he was one of them. The teachers did not seem to mind that he was just 12, they were talking to him as though it was a natural thing for him to be included in their group discussions. In fact they were amazed at the intensity of his knowledge and understanding, and impressed with his ability to speak at such a well-informed level. When Joseph and I saw this, I approached Jesus and reprimanded him for causing us to worry when we discovered he was not among the family members of the caravan, and for making it necessary for us to return to Jerusalem to find him. His response was, *"Why did you have to look for Me? Did you not know that I had to be in My Father's house about my Father's business?"* Instead of Joseph and I reprimanding him, he seemed to be reprimanding us although he did leave the Temple and return home with us as the obedient son he had always been; and he continued in his obedience and submission to us as his parents. But that incident is just an example of what I mean when I say I lived with an uncertainty of my parental authority.

Then Mary sat up a little straighter with her shoulders back, chest out, and head held high to continue her narrative.

There was the time, she said, when I took full advantage of my status as the mother of Jesus because I wanted to show off just a little bit. We were invited guests at a wedding in Cana and the host of the wedding celebration ran out of wine, so I told Jesus about it. He replied with another of his authoritative statements, *"What does that have to do with you and me? My time to act and to be revealed has not yet come."* But I ignored his statement and immediately told the servants of the house to listen carefully to my son and to do whatever he told them to do. Then I walked away and continued to converse with the other guests. Of course you know the rest of the story my sisters; that day, my son performed the first of his many miracles, he turned the hosts' purification water supply into fine wine. And that wine turned out to be the best and most excellent wine ever. Even the Steward of the house said so.

But the saddest and most distressful day of my entire life was the day my son was executed on a cross for crimes he did not commit. I cannot think of anything worse than a child dying before its mother; and worse yet is a mother helplessly witnessing firsthand the death of her child at the hands of murderous killers. At this point, Mary gasped, let out a most mournful groan and slumped into a heap on the floor sobbing and wailing uncontrollably. All of the women immediately rushed to her side embraced her and sobbed with her. As mothers themselves, they understood her pain. There were several moments of sobbing, wailing, groaning, swaying and expressions of deep and severe agony. Jennifer had not joined the women to embrace Mary, but she did begin to reflect on the price of Calvary, the cross, the crucifixion, and the shedding of blood. She remembered the scriptural passage in the book of Romans which says, *"all have sinned and fall short of the glory of God..."* Jennifer remembered further that the passage declared, *justification or being*

171

declared free of the guilt of sin happens as a result of the redemption that comes through Christ Jesus. Jennifer suddenly becomes acutely aware of the heart-wrenching significance of this passage as she witnesses firsthand Mary's agony. What a terrible experience for a mother to visually endure the unmerited and horrific crucifixion of her son; but what an amazing salvific privilege it provides for all of humanity. Jennifer begins to weep softly as she tries to comprehend this juxtaposition. The women, Mary included, hear Jennifer's whimpering's, and they all turn to her with compassion and embrace her. They seem to know exactly what she is thinking and feeling. Jennifer has never felt such overwhelming love as she feels from the collection of these beautiful and strong women. Finally, after several more minutes, the crying ceases and Mary attempts to move on with her story.

Mary addresses Jennifer. Jennifer, there is a very beautiful song that provokes much thought about me as the mother of the Messiah my son, and it's entitled, *Mary Did You Know*, written by a young man who lives in your 21st century. In his song the young man seems to have captured some of my own questions about life as the mother of my son Jesus our Lord and Savior. The song writer wants to know if I as Jesus's mother knew he would ever walk on water. I certainly did not give that a thought as I was raising him. The song also asks if I knew that the child I delivered would someday deliver me? A most powerful question that would have had no sense of meaning had I not seen him hanging on that cross. Here again Mary pauses, and drops her head in sorrowful position for a few more moments before continuing. Lifting her head she goes on; the song further asks if I knew that my son would give sight to the blind, calm raging storms, or restore hearing to the deaf. I must confess that I did not know all of these details about my

172

son. I simply knew what Gabriel told me, that I had found favor with God, that I would conceive a son by the overshadowing of the Holy Spirit and that my son would reign over the house of Jacob forever, that he would be great and be called the Son of the Highest. I don't recall any details about him being murderously crucified on a cross. But nonetheless, I have been highly favored by God and there is nothing greater or worthy of any comparison than to be favored and chosen by God. The room was still for a few moments of reverent silence because all the other women in the room knew exactly who Jesus was.

Then guardedly and almost fearfully, Jennifer broke the silence with a question she could no longer keep unasked, "Virgin Mary, may I ask you two questions?" Of course you may my dear, was Mary's response. "Virgin Mary, knowing the kind of truthful and trustworthy person you were did Joseph ever apologize to you for doubting you? Did he ever tell you that despite your story being quite a preposterous one, he should have believed it simply because you said it?" Mary glanced knowingly around the room at her sisters in history before replying to Jennifer's two questions with one answer; no my dear, he did not. As Jennifer mused Mary's answer for a few introspective moments the realization began to sink in that she had been given a tremendous amount of information to absorb in one night. She felt she was almost at the point of information-overload as she roamed the room with her eyes into the faces of these beautiful and brave women of antiquity who smiled knowingly at her as though they fully understood her thoughts and emotions. What an amazingly unbelievable night this has been!

Chapter 12
Now They Were Leaving

Jennifer was astounded, she was fascinated. She was spellbound. The stories of these women had riveted her attention from the moment they began to speak. She could only imagine how she must have looked; her head rotating in slow-motion from one to the other as she gazed with open mouth at these beautiful, strong, gentle, wise women who had shared their personal and painful life encounters with her.

Then Mary stood up, came and sat on Jennifer's bed, and gently turned Jennifer's face toward hers so they looked directly at each other, eye to eye. The other women gathered around as though knowing what Mary was about to say and wanting to demonstrate their individual and collective support of what was to come next. Mary addressed Jennifer in gentle but firm tones, "Jennifer my dear, we have one final message for you about a woman not nearly as old as we all are, and she too has a story to tell." There was a silent pause in the room as all the women nodded and smiled expressively at Jennifer with an air that suggested she might be the one Mary was speaking of. Surely Jennifer thought, they couldn't be referring to her. As though hearing Jennifer's unspoken thoughts, Hannah interrupted the silence, "Yes Jennifer, we are referring to you; do not doubt what you have been hearing from our God. He indeed has been speaking to you about sharing the good news of Jesus the Christ." How had Hannah known this, Jennifer pondered? She had told no one of her desires to minister; there was no one within her congregation or denomination to whom she could go for clarity about her thoughts and yearnings, but mostly her confusion. She was confused about her leanings toward ministry because she and the rest of the countless women within her denomination had been told it was completely out of the realm of possibility. Women were forbidden to preach or pastor, because the scriptures said women were not to

usurp authority over the man, but to be in silence.
Additionally, they were told, "God never called a woman to
preach." Thus a woman who dared step out of the will of God
to pastor would certainly be guilty of usurping authority over
her male congregants and clearly displeasing God. If
Jennifer's church upbringing and teachings were right, why
was she having such strong desires to minister, to attend
seminary, to preach the gospel, to perhaps one day pastor a
church? Where had those strong urges come from if not from
God? After all she was committed to the gospel, she was bold
enough to share it, she loved studying the scriptures and
desired more learning, she had a heart for humanity and she
was faithful in her desire to please God. Shouldn't those
aspects of her character be the determining factors for
ministry? Why then was her gender alone the one and only
deciding consideration against ministry beyond the
traditional positions of Missionary or keynote speaker for a
Women's Day event? As Jennifer was going deeper and
deeper in thought, Mary and the others all seemed to know
her contemplations, they were sympathetic to her quandary
but unwilling to sit idly by and watch her plunge herself
deeper into a self-defeating frame of mind. So Sarah spoke
out, "Jennifer dear, you have a story to tell and you must tell
it. You have a precious and abiding relationship with the
Lord and you are obligated to tell it." Then Mary reminded
Jennifer of the times Jennifer had felt the spirit of the Lord
Jesus urging her to minister. She reminded Jennifer of the
day the Lord had actually challenged Jennifer with the
question, "*Are you ministering for me or not?*" Jennifer was
shocked that Mary knew this. After all, Jennifer had been
alone in her car driving home from a fiery church service
when she heard those words from the Lord. At the time of
the incident, Jennifer was convinced she was hearing from
God and made a decision to accept her call to ministry. But
years of indoctrination to the contrary, along with her ever

increasing hesitancy, and the eventuality of passing time, had all prevented her from proceeding with her acceptance to the call. Hence, other life issues had crept in and diminished the profundity of that unique and special moment alone with the Lord in the car. But now these women of the far distant past were challenging her anew. Jennifer sat in amazement there in the quiet semi-darkness of her bedroom as these old women began to speak to her.

"Tell your story Jennifer," Hagar admonished.
"Yes my dear, we have been sent here by our Loving God to tell our stories to you and to encourage you to tell yours," Miriam urged.
"You are being liberated dear," Lot's wife declared.
"Yours is a story that needs to be heard," said Job's wife.
"Our God has intervened for you and blessed you in many ways," spoke Mary.
"Others need to hear your story, they are waiting for you to tell it," Eve voiced.
Still astounded. Still fascinated. Still spellbound. Jennifer sat motionless still trying to fathom all that had occurred that late night.

Then slowly, as when they first arrived, the women all began to speak in unison again and just as Jennifer had the first time, she heard, understood and distinguished their every word.

"Look, the sun is rising."
"It is almost morning."
"I think we have tired her."
"It is so much to absorb in one night."
"She looks exhausted."
"Will she be alright?"

179

"Of course she will."

"I hope we haven't weakened her."

"Of course we haven't."

"She is strong, remember?"

"Yes she is."

"She will be fine."

"She is so brave."

"And so precious."

"Come, it is time we left her."

"She needs her rest."

They all repositioned themselves again just as when they first appeared, at the foot of Jennifer's bed. And together in unison they said, "Good-bye my Dear. How lovely it was to share this night with you, we thank you for hearing us. Now be sure to tell our stories, it is very important that you do so."

And as mysteriously as they had appeared, they were gone. Jennifer looked around her room. It was so very empty now and she felt such a sad loneliness for those ancient and wonderful women who just a short while ago had lovingly filled her room with their warm and sweet presence. Jennifer's eyes welled with tears. Then in the quiet stillness with an ever-so-faint and far away tone, yet very clearly and with a commanding authority, Jennifer heard a gentle whisper of many unified voices speaking as one voice, "No sadness my dear, dry your eyes, just tell our stories. And be very certain to tell yours as well."

The Author, *Rev. Dr. Sheila Robinson*, is the granddaughter of a Pentecostal Pastor/Preacher and grew up entirely in the church. Currently she serves as Associate Pastor at Grace Tabernacle Community Church in San Francisco, CA under the pastorate of Bishop Ernest L. Jackson. Dr. Robinson holds an MA in Pastoral Ministries from Fuller Theological Seminary and a Doctor of Ministry from San Francisco Theological Seminary. She is also a Certified Life Coach.

With a 29-year broadcasting career, Sheila Robinson:
-Hosted a Sunday morning Gospel Music radio show and a
 Public Affairs Talk Show
-Hosted a weekly Community Channel TV Talk Show
-Co-founded the San Francisco Bay Area Religious Announcers Guild
-Is a 9-time Best Religious Announcer recipient from the Bay
 Area Gospel Academy Awards
-Was inducted into the Bay Area Gospel Academy Awards Hall of Fame

A published author and freelance writer, Sheila Robinson:
-Is a contributing writer for the *Women of Color Study Bible* -
Held radio interviews in Montego Bay and Kingston, Jamaica
for her book of poetry entitled, *My Perfect God*.
-Was recognized by the Peninsula Book Club for literary
excellence among local African American Writers.
-Authored a novel entitled, *Those Old Women: tell their stories*

With a heart for travel, Sheila Robinson:
-Was invited in 1995, by the Citizen Ambassador Program of
  People to People International, in conjunction with the China
  Women's Association for Science & Technology, to attend the
  US/China, Joint Conference on Women's Issues, in *Beijing,*
  China
-Applied her RN expertise by participating in the Rev.   Jackie
  McCullough, Medical & Evangelistic Outreach Crusade   in
  1999, in Ocho Rios, *Jamaica, West Indies*
-Traveled several times to the Hashemite Kingdom of *Jordan* in
  the Middle East visiting ancient Biblical sites and cities and was
  baptized in the Jordan River

Contact Information
Rev. Dr. Sheila Robinson can be contacted by email at
sheilafrob@gmail.com or by phone at 1.408.813.5043

Made in the USA
Columbia, SC
06 May 2018